Trouble with Lent

by
Paul McCusker

Augustine Institute
Greenwood Village, CO

Augustine Institute
6160 S. Syracuse Way, Suite 310
Greenwood Village, CO 80111
Tel: (866) 767-3155
www.augustineinstitute.org

Note: Different versions of some of these stories
have appeared in the *Signs of Grace* series.

Creative Director: Ben Dybas
Cover Design: Lisa Marie Patterson
Illustrations: Robert Dunn

ISBN-978-1-7335221-1-3
Library of Congress Control Number 2019931226

Printed in Canada

Contents

Introduction

Nicholas and Samantha Perry are twins. Nicholas is usually called Nick and Samantha is called Sam. They are both eight years old. They have a ten-year-old sister named Lizzy. Lizzy is short for Elizabeth. They also have a twelve-year-old brother named Andrew. Their parents are named Jon and Belle.

Nick and Sam have a good friend named Brad Wilkes. Brad comes to their house to play. He sometimes leads Nick and Sam into trouble.

Early last summer the Perry family moved from Denver to a town called Hope Springs. Hope Springs is near the

Rocky Mountains in Colorado. It is a town that has a lot of fun things to do.

Their church is called St. Clare of Assisi Catholic Church. Nick and Sam attend the church school next door. Father Cliff Montgomery is the new pastor at St. Clare's. He is young and full of energy. Sam says he is handsome. Nick says he is smart. Dad says he looks too young to be a pastor.

Deacon Chuck Crosby is older and helps Father Cliff a lot. Norm Sullivan is the handyman for the church and the adjoining school. He is friendly and has an unusual way of thinking about things.

Nick and Sam like Hope Springs. They visited relatives there when they were growing up. Now they are happy to live there.

Our stories tell about Nick's and Sam's life in Hope Springs. Maybe theirs is a lot like yours.

CHAPTER ONE

Pancakes & Promises

Nick looked down at the golden brown pancake on his plate. A smiley face of chocolate chips smiled back at him. He reached for the bowl that held more chocolate chips.

"Don't overdo it," his mom warned him.

The Perry family was sitting at the kitchen table for dinner. They didn't normally eat pancakes for dinner. This meal was special because it was "Shrove Tuesday." Shrove Tuesday was the day

when many Christians prepared for the season of Lent.

Nick's mom put pancakes on everyone's plates while they talked.

"Why is it called Shrove Tuesday?" Nick's twin sister Sam asked. "I don't remember."

Nick's father looked at Andrew and Lizzy. Andrew was Nick's oldest brother. Lizzy was Nick's older sister. "One of you two should answer," he said.

Lizzy said, "The word 'shrove' means 'absolve.'"

"What does the word 'absolve' mean?" he asked.

Andrew said, "It means 'to be forgiven' or 'to be set free from guilt.' Just like we are absolved by the priest when we go to Confession."

"Very good," Mrs. Perry said.

"Pass the syrup," Nick asked Sam, then remembered to add "please."

Sam passed the bottle of syrup and

groaned. "You're going to put syrup on *that?*"

"Yep." Nick began to squeeze syrup all over the chocolate-chip-smiley-face pancake.

Nick flexed his left hand. He moved his wrist back and forth. He had been wearing a cast on his wrist for almost two months because of a fall he'd taken.[1] The doctor took the cast off that morning.

"How does it feel?" Mr. Perry asked.

"Kind of stiff," Nick said.

"The doctor gave you a sheet of special exercises to do," Mrs. Perry reminded him. "You have to start right away. We'll take you to a physical therapist next week."

"It seems okay to me." Nick picked up his fork and took a big bite of his pancake.

---

[1] For that story, read *The Adventures of Nick & Sam 3: The Best Advent Ever*

"In the name of the Father, the Son, and the Holy Spirit," Mr. Perry said as he did the Sign of the Cross.

Nick froze. He had forgotten to wait to pray.

"Bless us, O Lord, and these thy gifts, which we are about to receive from thy bounty," the rest of the family said together. Nick mumbled. Then they finished with the Sign of the Cross again.

Nick didn't look at the others. He chewed his pancake again.

"What do pancakes have to do with being forgiven?" Mr. Perry asked.

Andrew shifted in his chair. "People used to give up things like eggs and milk and flour and sugar for Lent. So they used up their supply on Shrove Tuesday."

"Because tomorrow is Ash Wednesday," Lizzy added. "And that's when Lent really begins."

Mrs. Perry said, "Your father and I have decided what we will give up for Lent this year."

Nick looked up. He hoped it wasn't going to be anything too hard.

"We're going to give up the television," his mom said.

Mr. Perry looked around the table. "Have you decided what you're giving up for Lent?"

Nick took another bite. He hadn't thought about it at all, even though Sister Lucy, his teacher, kept reminding them to.

"I'm giving up math," Andrew said.

The family laughed.

"Or, I'll give up watching television, too," he added.

"What about you, Lizzy?" Mr. Perry asked.

"I'm going to give up reading books that aren't about my faith," Lizzy said.

"Sam?"

Sam took a bite of bacon. "I'm going to give up eating hamburgers," she said.

Nick knew he was next. He didn't know what he should give up. He didn't want to give up anything.

His father coaxed him. "Nick?"

Nick looked down at his pancake. "I haven't decided."

"You should give up sweets," Sam said.

Nick shot a look at her.

"That's a good idea," Mrs. Perry said.

"Forty days without sweets?" Andrew said. "He can't do it."

Nick looked at his brother. "I can if I decide to do it."

"It's the healthy thing to do," said Mr. Perry. He thought for a moment. "How about this? I'll give up sweets if you will. We can help each other."

All eyes were on Nick. He wiggled in his chair.

"He can't do it," Andrew said again.

"I can too!"

"Don't tease him," Mrs. Perry said to Andrew. "It's his choice."

"Remember: we don't fast during Lent just to fast," Mr. Perry said. "We do it to get things out of the way of our relationship with God."

Mrs. Perry said to Nick, "You don't have to decide right now."

Nick looked at Andrew like he'd taken a dare. "I'm giving up sweets," he declared.

"So will I," Mr. Perry said.

Nick grabbed some chocolate chips from the bowl and dropped them onto the last portion of his pancake.

"Ew," Sam said.

"That's enough," said his mom.

Nick smiled. "I better eat them while I can."

Later, Nick got ready for bed. His mind was racing. He felt twitchy because of all of the chocolate and syrup. He put on his pajamas and paced around his room.

He saw the sheet of exercises for his wrist sitting on his bed.

One exercise had him put his arm on a table and make a fist then move his fist up and down ten times as far as he could. Others had him put his palms up and down and straight out and around and bent this way and that five times and ten times and—

Nick tossed the sheet on his desk. *I don't need to do all of these. My wrist feels okay*, he thought.

CHAPTER TWO

Ashes & Bees

Early the next morning the family went to the Ash Wednesday Mass at St. Clare of Assisi Catholic Church. It was like a regular Mass but had a special part where Father Cliff and Deacon Chuck pressed ashes onto everyone's forehead.

"Ashes remind us that we are sinners who need Jesus Christ," Father Cliff said in his homily. "We know our need for his mercy, love, and forgiveness. We soften our hearts to him. We are penitent."

The Perry family got in line to receive the ashes. Sam hoped that Deacon Chuck would put the ashes on her forehead. Her best friend Kim said he made the ashes look like a cross. Father Cliff made them look like a dark gray smudge.

Sam wound up with the dark gray smudge. Nick's looked like an "X." Lizzy's looked like a cross. Andrew's looked like a dash. Her dad's looked like a half circle. Her mom's looked like a comma.

The kids called out "goodbye" to their parents and walked across the grounds to St. Clare's Catholic School. A light snow fell on them. Nick made the mistake of wiping at the snowflakes that hit his forehead. It smeared the ashes even more.

"You look like a coal miner," Andrew teased him.

Sam and Nick were in the same class.

Their teacher, Sister Lucy, was a young woman with a round face and a ready smile. She wore a long white robe that went all the way down to her shoes. A white cape covered her shoulders and she wore a black veil over her light brown hair. The black veil had a white band that held it on her head. She also wore a silver crucifix around her neck and a large rosary on her belt.

Sister Lucy handed out forms for the students to take home. "We are going to take a special field trip next week," she announced. "Your parents need to sign the forms or you can't go."

Sam looked down at the form. It stated that the two third-grade classes were taking a bus to the Great Sand Dunes National Park. Sam remembered that the Sand Dunes were an odd patch of desert somewhere south of Hope Springs. Her dad had said that it was like the wind had picked up sand from a faraway desert and blew it into a corner of the Colorado mountains.

Sister Stephanie appeared in the doorway. Sister Stephanie was the principal of the school. She signaled to Sister Lucy.

"I'll be right back," Sister Lucy said as she went out into the hall.

The students looked at one another. Sam wondered if they were going to have a school drill. A moment later, Sister Lucy returned with a boy behind her. The boy had light brown hair that seemed to stick up in different directions. He had a freckled face and lines between his eyes that made him look like he was thinking hard. He was wearing his winter coat and carried a backpack.

Sister Lucy put a hand on the boy's shoulder. "Class, we have a new student joining us today. His name is Riley Switzer. He recently moved here

from Wyoming. Make sure to welcome him." She pointed to the closets at the back of the class. "Riley, you can hang your coat in the closet and sit there— at that desk next to Nick."

Riley disappeared behind the closets.

Sam looked at Nick. Nick looked at the empty desk next to him.

Sam watched as Riley dropped into the chair and put his backpack at his feet.

"Hi," Nick said to him.

Riley gave him a toothy smile. "Do you like Big Foot?" he asked loudly.

Some of the kids laughed.

"I haven't thought about him much," Nick said.

"You're interested in the legends of Big Foot?" Sister Lucy asked him.

"Oh *yes*," he said. Then he looked very serious. "But it's not a legend."

Sister Lucy smiled. "Maybe you can do a report for us one day," she said.

"All right, everyone, take out your math homework from last night.

Sam caught Nick's eye. He had an expression that said, *I'm sitting next to a kid who believes in Big Foot?*

Later that morning, Sister Lucy talked about the season of Lent. She explained how Christians all over the world used that time to help people in need. Then she went over a story that Jesus told years ago about the Good Samaritan.

She told them that the Samaritans were a group of people that lived in the nation of Israel with the Jews. The Jews and Samaritans didn't get along with each other. Sometimes they fought. Most of the time they ignored each other.

One day, Jesus told his followers about a man who was walking along a road when suddenly robbers attacked him. They took all the man had, beat him, and left him in a ditch.

Later, a Jewish priest was walking along the road and saw the man lying in the ditch. He made sure to move to the far side of the road to avoid the man. After that, a religious worker came along. He saw the man in the ditch and also passed by on the far side of the road.

Then came a Samaritan. He saw the man in the ditch and went over to him. He gave the man ointments for his wounds and bandaged him up. Then he put the man on his mule and carried him to an inn. He gave the innkeeper a lot of money and told him to take good care of the man. At the end of the story Jesus told his listeners to show mercy like the Samaritan did.

Sister Lucy told the class to write down ways they could show mercy to others.

"I would show mercy to Big Foot," Riley said loudly. "I wouldn't put him in a cage like some people want to do."

"Write it down, Riley," Sister Lucy said. "We'll talk about that another time."

Sam wrote down "soup kitchen." She decided then to ask her parents about volunteering at St. Clare's soup kitchen for the poor.

Sister Lucy dismissed the class for lunch. The students chatted as they got up from their desks. Sam was talking to her best friend, Kim, when Sister Lucy said, "Sam, I need to talk to you."

Kim nodded and went out to the hall. Sam went to Sister Lucy's desk at the front of the room.

"Yes, Sister?" Sam asked.

"We have our school spelling bee coming up," Sister Lucy said. "A student from every class competes. I would like you to take part."

Sam's heart pounded. "Me?"

"You're the best speller in our class," said Sister Lucy.

"What will I have to do?" Sam asked.

Sister Lucy handed her a sheet of paper. "These are the rules and form

for your parents to give their okay. We'll have rounds every Friday during the morning assembly. The last one will be the Wednesday of Holy Week, before our Easter break."

"Will I know the words?" Sam asked.

"Two days before each round we'll give you a hundred words to look over," Sister Lucy said.

Sam gasped. "A *hundred*?"

"You won't have to spell all of them," Sister Lucy explained. "You will be asked to spell only five of the hundred. But you won't know which five."

"When does it start?" Sam asked.

"This Friday morning," Sister Lucy said. "That's why I'm giving you the list of a hundred words now." She handed Sam another sheet of paper.

Sam looked down. She saw words like "about" and "across" and "until" and "Wednesday."

"Will you do it?" Sister Lucy asked.

Sam looked at her teacher and smiled. "Yes," she said.

Sam stepped into the hall and looked for Kim. Suddenly Lance Smith stepped up to her. He had a big grin on his face.

Sam took a step back. Lance was the kind of boy who always stood too close when he talked. He had big brown eyes and teeth that looked too big for his mouth. Lance also had a crush on Sam. She was afraid he might try to kiss her. He did it before. In front of a lot of people. She punched him for it.[2]

"Did Sister Lucy talk to you about the spelling bee?" Lance asked.

"Yes," Sam replied.

"I told her to ask you to do it," Lance said proudly.

---

[2] For that story, read *The Adventures of Nick & Sam 3: The Best Advent Ever*

"Oh." Sam wasn't sure what to do. "Thank you."

"I know you'll win," Lance said.

"I hope so," Sam said.

Lance put out his hand.

Sam flinched. Then she realized he wanted her to shake it. So she did. It was a squishy handshake.

He chuckled and walked away.

Kim stood nearby. She grinned at Sam.

Sam rolled her eyes.

"What did he want?" Kim asked.

"He said it was his idea for Sister Lucy to put me in the spelling bee," she said.

"You're in the spelling bee?" Kim asked.

Sam nodded.

Kim gave a little squeak of joy and jumped up and down with excitement.

CHAPTER THREE

Eyelids & Big Foot

"You gave up *what?*" Brad asked Nick at lunch.

They were sitting at a table. Sister Penelope had just led everyone in the blessing. Nick then told Brad about his promise for Lent.

"You're giving up sweets? *All* sweets?" Brad asked. "Like chocolate and cupcakes and ice cream sandwiches and those really good candy bars that are filled with caramel and—"

"Stop it," Nick said. He knew Brad was teasing him.

"Was it your idea?" Brad asked.

"Yes."

Brad leaned back in his seat. He shook his head. "You're not supposed to give up things you really like. You're supposed to give up things people *think* you like. Then it's not so hard."

"What are you giving up?" Nick asked.

"Video games," Brad said. He took a bite of his sandwich.

Nick was shocked. "But you *love* video games!"

"It was my parents' idea," Brad said with a frown. "I wanted to give up *carrots*."

With a loud crash, Sam dropped her lunch tray onto the table. "I really miss hamburgers," she said.

"You miss them?" Brad asked.

Nick said to Brad, "She gave up hamburgers for Lent."

Brad laughed.

"It's not funny," Sam grumbled. She sat across from Nick and picked up her sandwich. "What is this?"

"Some kind of egg salad," Kim said as she put down her lunch bag. She slid into a seat next to Sam.

"What are you giving up?" Sam asked her.

"Noodles," Kim said.

"Noodles?" Brad asked.

"*Noodles*, like the noodles you put in soup," Kim said. "I'm Chinese and my family loves noodles. I could eat noodles all day."

Nick was tired of talking about food. His gaze drifted over to another table. Riley, the new kid, was about to sit down with his lunch bag. Sam also saw him.

"There's Riley. We should invite him over," Sam said.

Brad glanced over. "Maybe he wants to sit by himself," Brad suggested.

"No one likes to sit alone in a new

school," Sam said. "Don't forget the Good Samaritan story."

Sam got up and went over to talk to Riley. A moment later Riley was sitting next to Nick at the table.

Riley opened his lunch bag. He brought out a plastic bag with a sandwich, a banana, a bag of chips, and a plastic cup with a lid and spoon. There was chocolate pudding in the cup.

Chocolate. Nick groaned.

Suddenly Riley looked at them and said, "I can turn my eyelids inside out. Do you want to see?"

The girls said "no." The boys said "yes."

Riley reached up and fiddled with his eyelids until the pink on the inside faced out. The girls screeched. The boys laughed.

Riley blinked a couple of times and his eyes went back to normal. He took out his sandwich and began to eat.

Brad leaned on the table. "Why were you talking about Big Foot in class?" he asked.

Kim said, "I don't know what Big Foot is."

Riley reached into his pocket. He took out a mangled piece of paper. He spread it out in front of Kim. "That's Big Foot," he said.

On the paper was a drawing of a large beast. It had the body of a human but was covered with hair like a gorilla. Its face looked like a man's but the forehead was really high. Long hair sprung out from under its eyes and around its mouth.

"That's a *yeran*," Kim said. "Some people call it a 'yeti.' A 'man-monkey.' A 'Chinese wild-man.'"

Riley looked at Kim like he'd just made a new friend. "The Chinese Big Foot has been seen in the mountains of western..." Riley struggled with what he was trying to say. "...Hoo-bye."

"Hubei is in the middle of China," Kim said. "I have cousins there."

"Will you ask them to send pictures of your Big Foot?" Riley asked.

"My left or my right?" Kim teased.

Nick thought that was funny.

Riley didn't get the joke. He pulled another piece of paper from another pocket. This one was a newspaper clipping.

The headline announced, "Local Big Foot Sighting."

Next to the headline was a blurry photo of a man named John Hunter. He wore a big furry hat and large furry coat. He was pointing to something on the bark of a tree.

Riley said, "John Hunter saw Big Foot up in the mountains. He found claw marks on a tree near a place called the Little Big Pond."

Nick had been to the Little Big Pond for a picnic with his family. It was really a big lake.

Brad shook his head. "I've heard about John Hunter. He's crazy. He believes in spaceships. And he said he saw a giant monster in a lake in Wyoming."

"Does Wyoming have lakes?" Nick asked.

"I wish I could meet him," Riley said. He ate his sandwich in four big bites.

Sam stared at Riley. "I have never seen anyone eat so fast," she said.

Riley blushed.

"Mr. Norm probably knows John Hunter," Nick said. "He knows *everybody* in town."

Riley's eyes lit up. "Who is Mr. Norm? Can we talk to him?"

Nick shrugged. "He's the handyman here. He's always around somewhere. Maybe we'll see him when we go out for recess."

Riley picked up the plastic cup. He looked at it and frowned. "*Chocolate* pudding? I don't like chocolate," he said. "Does anybody want this?"

The kids at the table looked at Nick.

Nick felt his mouth water. "No, thanks." He looked away.

"I'll eat it," Brad said.

He made it a point to reach across Nick to get the cup from Riley. He took off the top and began to eat very loudly with a lot of "hmm" and "mmm" noises. Just for Nick.

Sometimes Nick didn't like Brad very much.

Nick, Brad, and Riley walked back to their class to get their hats and coats for recess. Along the way, Brad said, "I'll see you later" and went off to a different hall.

"Where are you going?" Nick called out.

Brad shouted back, "I have something to do."

Nick and Riley walked on. "Is he your best friend?" Riley asked.

"Yeah," said Nick.

"Can we be best friends?" Riley asked.

Nick wasn't sure how to answer the

question. He finally offered a "maybe."

The two boys put on their hats and coats. They went out to the playground next to the school. It was warm in the bright sunshine. There were still patches of snow on the ground from the last snowfall.

Nick looked for Brad. He was nowhere to be seen.

"Is that Mr. Norm?" Riley asked. He pointed to a wooden shed.

Mr. Norm stood outside of the shed. He wore a big overcoat and hunter's cap.

"That's him," Nick said.

They walked over. Mr. Norm nodded to them. He took a toothpick that stuck out from one side of his mouth and tucked it in the other side.

"Hi, Mr. Norm," Nick called out. "This is Riley."

"The new boy," Mr. Norm said. "Nice to meet you."

"Have you ever seen Big Foot?" Riley asked him.

Mr. Norm chuckled. "Only when I put on my shoes."

Riley dug into his pockets and showed Mr. Norm his newspaper clipping.

"Do you know John Hunter?" Riley asked him.

"He's an old friend," said Mr. Norm. "He has a *huge* collection of Big Foot stuff in his house."

Riley brightened. "Can we see it?"

Mr. Norm gave it some thought. "John tends to keep to himself. But I'll ask."

"Thank you!" Riley said.

Nick thought about going to the house. "John Hunter isn't crazy, is he?"

Mr. Norm touched the toothpick on his lip. "He gets his mind fixed on certain things and can't let go of them."

"Do *you* believe in Big Foot?" asked Riley.

Mr. Norm took the toothpick out of his mouth. "I believe the world still has a lot of mysteries that we haven't solved. Maybe there are big creatures hiding out there. Maybe they don't want us to find them. I respect that."

The boys said thanks and goodbye. Mr. Norm tapped a hand to his forehead like a salute. He stepped into the shed and began poking around.

Nick saw Brad in the doorway to the school. He was looking up at Mr. Hildreth, one of the gym teachers. Mr. Hildreth was jabbing a finger in the air. Brad looked like he was in trouble. He nodded to Mr. Hildreth. Brad came outside.

Nick walked up to him. "What happened?" he asked.

"Nothing," Brad said.

"Were you in trouble?" Riley asked.

"I don't want to talk about it," Brad said.

"We talked to Mr. Norm about John Hunter!" Riley exclaimed.

Brad didn't seem to care. "Good for you," he said. He stormed away from them to the playset area.

Nick wondered what was wrong with his friend.

CHAPTER FOUR

Words & Fevers

Sam paced in her room at home. She held the long list of spelling bee words in her hand.

Why did they give me so many? she wondered. *Do I really have to learn them all?*

She took the list to her small study desk. She decided to cross off the words she already knew. After that, she had only fifty words she wasn't sure about.

But fifty is still a lot, she thought. *Raised ... Finished ... Stretch ... Laugh ... Wednesday ...*

Her dad stepped into the doorway. "Dinner's in a half hour," he said.

"Okay." She frowned at the list.

He came into the room. "Homework?"

"Spelling bee words," Sam griped.

"Your mom told me about that," her dad said. "It's an honor that Sister Lucy thought you could do it."

She held the list up for her dad to look. "I crossed off the words I know."

He looked over the list. "A lot of these words have to do with Lent."

"They do?"

"Fasting, Easter, Penance ..." he read out loud. "Here's a hard one."

He pointed to a long word on the page.

"Abstinence," he said out loud. "I always get the 'e' and the 'a' confused in words that end with 'ence' and 'ance.'"

Sam did, too. She said the word slowly. "*Ab-stin-ence.*"

"It comes from the word 'abstain,'" her father said. "You are *abstaining* from eating hamburgers during Lent. *Abstinence* is the bigger word for that."

Sam shook her head. "I'm already sorry I gave up hamburgers for Lent. They're all I can think about," she said.

He smiled. "Giving something up usually makes us want it more. But it's good for us to sacrifice what we want."

Sam thought that was the kind of thing parents always said.

"It's like learning all those words." He waved a hand at the list. "It's good to know more than we think we need to know." He looked like he hadn't said what he meant to say. He tried again. "I mean, learning to be a good learner is as important as what you're learning."

Sam giggled.

Mr. Perry laughed. "You know what I mean."

Just then, her mom came to the door.

She looked worried. "Something's wrong with Lizzy."

Sam followed her parents to Lizzy's room. The door was open, but Mrs. Perry still tapped on the doorframe. "Lizzy?" she half-whispered.

The room was dark. A weak voice said, "Come in."

Sam followed her parents in. Lizzy was under her covers. She looked like she was sleeping.

"Taking a nap?" Mr. Perry asked. He sat down on her bed.

"I got really tired," Lizzy said in a soft voice. "I don't know why. My body aches."

Mrs. Perry put a hand on Lizzy's forehead. "You have a fever," Mrs. Perry said. She looked at her husband. "I want to take her to the clinic."

"So soon?" asked Mr. Perry. "Give it a couple of days to run its course."

Mrs. Perry shook her head. "I heard that a couple of kids in Lizzy's class are sick. If I take her to the doctor's sooner, then maybe they can give her something to fight it off."

Sam's sister looked like she could hardly walk on her own. Her face was pale but her cheeks were flushed. Mrs. Perry half-carried Lizzy to the car in the garage.

"I don't know how long we'll have to wait," Mrs. Perry said. "Don't let dinner get cold."

"I'll save some for you," Mr. Perry called after her.

Mrs. Perry stepped into the garage. A minute later Sam heard the garage door go up and the car pull away.

Sam, her dad, Nick, and Andrew sat down to their Ash Wednesday meal: tomato soup, bread, and salad. Sam thought about hamburgers again. Mr. Perry prayed for the food and for Lizzy.

The tomato soup reminded Sam of her Good Samaritan idea.

"Can we help serve food at the St. Clare soup kitchen?" Sam asked.

Her father had just put a spoonful of soup in his mouth. He swallowed and then said, "That's a great idea."

"All of us?" Nick asked.

"Sure," his dad said. "We're supposed to help the poor during Lent."

Sam was pleased.

Nick said, "Oh! I almost forgot!" He told them about Riley and Big Foot and John Hunter.

Mr. Perry stabbed at his salad. "John Hunter? He's still chasing after the Sasquatch?"

"Sasquatch?" Nick asked.

"It's another name for Big Foot," his father said.

Andrew tore up a slice of bread. He dropped the chunks into his soup. Sam watched them turn red. "I found stuff online about John Hunter and Big Foot," said Andrew.

"Why were you looking him up?" Mr. Perry asked.

"I've been reading a lot about local history," Andrew replied. "John Hunter is a member of the Nuche Nation," Andrew said.

"I think it's now called the Ute Nation," Mr. Perry said.

Andrew went on, "He was known as a tracker. His name in the tribe is Prancing Bear."

"If his name is Prancing Bear, then why is he called John Hunter?" Sam asked.

"That's his English name," Andrew said. "A lot of Native Americans took English names for legal reasons. I guess it made their lives easier."

Mr. Perry said, "He's been around as long as I can remember. He looked old when I was a kid."

"What about Big Foot?" Nick asked.

"An article said that John Hunter

first saw Big Foot when he was a young boy. He's been searching for it ever since," Andrew said.

Nick turned to his father. "Mr. Norm said John Hunter has a giant Big Foot display at his house. He's going to see if we can look at it. Is that okay?"

"I suppose so," Mr. Perry said with a nod. "I'd like to go along. I haven't seen John Hunter in a long time."

Nick went to his room to do homework. He looked at the exercises for his wrist.

There are too many, he thought. He moved his wrist up and down, then back and forth a couple of times. It felt stiff.

"That's enough," he said. He shoved the list away.

He heard his mom in the hallway. "I'll bring you something to drink in a minute," she said.

"Thank you," he heard Lizzy say.

He went to his bedroom door. He saw his mom help Lizzy into her room. She came back out a minute later.

"Family meeting!" she called out.

Everyone except Lizzy gathered in the family room. "Lizzy has mono," Mrs. Perry said.

Mr. Perry groaned.

Nick was confused. "What's mono?" he asked.

"Mono-nu-cle-osis," Mrs. Perry said slowly. "It's a virus that makes you really tired. Sometimes you have a fever and sore throat. Sometimes it lasts for a couple of weeks, sometimes longer."

"She'll miss school for that long?" Nick asked.

"Yes," said his mother. "It's highly contagious."

"You mean, *we'll* get it?" Sam asked.

"Not if we're very careful," Mrs. Perry said. "Don't go in her room. Don't touch things that she's touched. Stay away from anything she eats or drinks. Wash your hands a lot."

"Any idea how she got it?" Mr. Perry asked.

"Lizzy thinks she drank from the same cup as another girl in her class," said Mrs. Perry. "I called Sister Stephanie about it. That girl has mono too."

"How is Lizzy feeling now?" Sam asked.

"She's feverish and tired," Mrs. Perry said. "All she wants to do is sleep."

"Is there anything can we do for her?" Mr. Perry asked.

Mrs. Perry answered, "She needs to drink a lot of water and juice. I'll make some chicken noodle soup. Mostly we need to leave her alone to rest."

CHAPTER FIVE

Notes & Nibbles

Sam had a hard time concentrating at school the next day. She was worried about Lizzy at home with mono. She also kept thinking about the spelling bee words. Sister Lucy had to get after her for looking at the spelling bee list when she was supposed to be doing her math.

Some of the words were hard for Sam to spell. "Wednesday" always confused her.

Kim helped Sam practice the

words during lunch. She had to spell "Wednesday" three times before she got it right.

In the afternoon, Sister Lucy told the class to draw pictures of things that reminded them of Lent.

Nick drew a picture of a chocolate bar.

Sam drew a picture of an angel standing on a rock.

Kim was sitting next to her and asked, "What does it mean?"

"This is the angel that helped Jesus in the desert," Sam said. "I'm going to give it to Lizzy."

At the end of the school day, Sam went to get her coat from the class closet. She saw a piece of paper sticking out of the pocket. She pushed it in deeper so it wouldn't fall out.

When she got home, she found the note in her pocket again. She thought it might be from Kim. She shoved the note into her backpack and carried it up to her room.

She took out her drawing of the angel in the desert. She went to Lizzy's room and knocked on the door.

"Come in," Lizzy said. She sounded very tired.

Sam walked in. The curtains were drawn. The room was dark. Lizzy lay on her bed.

"How are you feeling?" Sam asked.

"Okay," Lizzy said.

Even in the dim light Sam saw that Lizzy's cheeks were red. Her eyes looked half their normal size.

"I brought you something," Sam said. She handed her the drawing of the angel.

"Thank you," said Lizzy. "That's so sweet."

"Do you know what it is?"

"The angel that fed Jesus in the desert?" Lizzy asked.

Sam was surprised. "That's right! How did you know?" Sam asked.

"It looks like a desert. And the rock has the shadow of Jesus on it," she said. She held up the picture.

Sam got closer, but not too close. There was a shadow on the rock of a man. He looked like he was kneeling.

Sam looked at Lizzy. "I didn't draw that shadow."

"But it's there," Lizzy said.

Sam shook her head. "Why do strange things always seem to happen with you?"

"They don't seem strange to me," Lizzy said.

A few months ago, Sam learned that Lizzy sometimes saw her guardian angel. She even drew pictures of him. That was a big surprise. Their parents and Lizzy talked to Father Cliff about it. Father Cliff was sure it was an angel and not something else.

"Some of the saints saw amazing things," he had told them.

They all agreed not to talk about it outside of the family.

"Has your angel come to visit you since you got sick?" Sam asked Lizzy.

Lizzy closed her eyes. "I thought I saw him last night. But that might have been my fever. I'm sure he's around somewhere."

Nick sat at the desk in his room. He had to do a worksheet about periods and commas and question marks.

His eye fell on the exercise sheet for his wrist. He picked it up.

Not now, he thought. He turned it over and put it down again.

He grabbed the worksheet from school. He needed a pencil to do it. Where was his pencil?

He opened the desk drawer. There was a lot of junk in it. He pushed past

some paper clips and a small plastic pencil sharpener and marbles and little soldiers and gum wrappers and playing cards. His hand brushed against something that made a crinkle sound. He pushed an index card aside and uncovered a Choco-Nut-Nibble candy bar. It was one of his favorites. He picked it up. "Peanuts," the wrapper said, and "Caramel" and "Chocolatey Goodness."

He lifted the bar and looked at it in the lamplight.

He imagined how good it would taste.

He looked at the open door behind him. No one was around.

No one would know.

Sam went back to her room. It wasn't until she had finished her history homework that she thought of the note. She took it out of her backpack. It was folded up. She carefully undid it.

The page was the list of spelling bee words. Some of the words were circled.

There was a handwritten message at the bottom. "This will help you," it said.

These must be the words they want me to spell! she thought. She looked away before she saw the circled words. She quickly folded the paper up again.

Who would give me the answers? she wondered. *Maybe it's a prank. Maybe somebody wants me to think about the wrong words.*

She held the paper in her hand. It was hard to think. She was curious about which words were circled.

It's cheating! she told herself.

She tore the paper up into little pieces and dropped it into the trash can.

Problem solved, she thought. But she wondered again about who had given her the list.

Just then Nick walked into her room. He went over to her desk and dropped something on top.

"Hide that where I won't find it," he said.

He turned and walked out again.

Sam took a closer look at what Nick had dropped.

It was a candy bar.

CHAPTER SIX

Spelling & Sneaking

It was Friday, the morning of the first round of the spelling bee. Sam was told to sit on the front row of the chairs with the other contestants.

The entire school was there for the morning assembly. Sam's mother also came. Her father stayed home with Lizzy. Mrs. Perry sat in the chairs in the middle of the hall with Andrew and Nick. Brad sat next to Nick. Kim waved to her from the other side of the room.

Father Cliff led the morning prayer. Then he talked about how Jesus spent forty days in the wilderness. "That is why some of us are taking a field trip to the Great Sand Dunes next week. It will give us an idea of what the wilderness was like for Jesus."

Father Cliff explained that a time of being alone is a time to become holy. "We get rid of our distractions. We focus on our relationship with God. That's why we make the forty days of Lent like Jesus's forty days in the wilderness," he said. "It helps us get rid of the things that distract us from God. It is also a time of temptation. Satan works hard to tempt us away from loving God. He tests us just like he tested Jesus. But Jesus was ready. Jesus had prayed. Jesus knew his mission. Jesus knew his Bible. So when Satan tested him, Jesus knocked Satan back with the Truth."

The contestants were led on stage after Father Cliff finished his talk. She was given a sign to hang around her neck by a string. It said "Samantha." Sister Lucy directed her to a row of folding chairs on the stage. All the contestants from the different grades had seats. She sat down next to Karl Enslow. Karl was from the other third-grade class. Sam knew that he was a very smart boy. He also liked to win.

"I'm going to win," Karl said and smiled at her.

Mr. Norm walked on stage and put two microphones on two stands. One was put on the left side and the other on the right side. The audience applauded him. He laughed and did a small bow.

Sister Stephanie sat down at a table in front of the stage. She tapped a microphone there.

"Good morning, students," she said to the kids on the stage.

Some of them said "good morning."

Sister Stephanie turned and explained to the crowd that each class had one contestant. That's why there were sixteen students on the stage. Two for each grade. She would begin with the first graders and work her way up to eighth grade. Ten words were chosen to fit the level of the grade.

She waved to a woman on her left and a man on her right. "Mrs. Craft and Mr. Landers have volunteered to monitor the words and the spellings, just to make sure everything is as it should be."

Mrs. Craft and Mr. Landers turned and bowed slightly. They were parents of a couple of the students.

"I know you'll be tempted," Sister Stephanie continued, "but *do not* help the students. No clues. No hints. No suggestions. No matter how much you want to."

Some of the parents laughed.

Sam felt nervous. She began to twist the bottom of her school sweater.

Sister Stephanie turned to the kids on the stage. "Did you study your words?" she asked.

"Yes, Sister," the kids said.

"You will be given a word," she said. "You may ask me to repeat the word. You may ask me to use the word in a sentence. You may ask me if there is another way to say the word. Do you understand?"

The kids said yes.

She went on: "After I say the word, please repeat the word back to me— spell the word clearly—then say the word again. Do you understand?"

Again the kids said yes.

She smiled at them. "Good. Then let's begin with the first graders."

Sam watched as the two first graders went to the two microphones. They seemed so little. The words were simple, like "go" and "yes" and "you" and "big." Both of the first graders spelled the words correctly.

Then the second graders stepped up to the microphones. They had words like "brown" and "job" and "fox" and "chase" and "shake." A boy from the second grade spelled the word drain as "d-r-a-n-e." Sister Stephanie thanked him and he left the stage.

The audience applauded for him.

She beckoned Sam and Karl to come to the microphones. Sam realized she had twisted her sweater out of shape. She tried to smooth it out when she stood up. Karl went to the microphone on the left. Sam went to the microphone on the right.

She wondered if there was a patron saint for spelling. *Please help me, whoever you are,* she thought.

"Ready?" Sister Stephanie asked them.

"Yes," Sam and Karl said. Sam thought her voice sounded too loud. It seemed to boom in the hall. She took a step back.

Sister Stephanie went back and forth between Sam and Karl, starting with Karl. He had to spell the words "fast" and "trouble" and "voice" and "absent" and "diagram." On two words he asked her to use the word in a sentence. Karl spelled them all correctly.

Then Sister Stephanie asked Sam to spell "Lent" and "branch" and "toddler" and "misfit" and, finally, "daughter."

Sam paused on the word "daughter." She said, "D-A-W"—and then stopped herself. "I'm sorry, D-A-U-G-H-T-E-R."

"That's correct," Sister Stephanie said.

The audience applauded as Sam and Karl sat down again.

Sam sat back. She was glad that was over. Her mom smiled at her.

"Good job," Karl whispered to her. "They'll be a lot harder next week."

Sam gave a small groan.

Nick was getting annoyed. Riley kept leaning over to talk to him during class. He also passed notes about Big Foot.

"Stop," Nick whispered to Riley.

"I can't help it," Riley whispered back. "I'm so excited. Aren't you excited?"

"Shh" Nick said.

"Do I have to separate you boys?" Sister Lucy asked.

Nick shot Riley a hard look. "No, Sister," he said.

Riley kept talking about Big Foot at lunch. Brad tried to change the subject. Nick couldn't think of a nice way to tell him to stop. Finally, Brad got up and left them.

"Where are you going?" Nick asked.

"I have some things to do," Brad said. He walked away.

Riley followed Nick outside to recess. Nick turned to Riley and said, "I need to talk to Brad alone."

Riley looked hurt. He went to the playsets and sat alone.

Nick looked around for Brad. He looked in all the places Brad liked to play. No Brad. Nick wondered if Brad went to the nurse for some reason. He walked back towards the door and then saw Brad huddled in a corner. He walked over. Brad had his back to the playground.

"Why are you hiding?" Nick asked.

Brad jumped with a small screech. He shoved a handheld video game into his coat pocket. "I'm not doing anything."

Nick laughed. "You were playing a video game."

Brad stood up and looked around. "Don't talk so loud."

"Why? What's wrong?" Nick asked.

"I told my parents I would give up playing games for Lent." Brad leaned against the wall. "But I didn't mean it," he said.

"That's cheating," Nick said.

"They *made* me do it, so it doesn't count," Brad said.

Nick thought about it, then said, "Yes it does."

Brad ignored him.

"Is that why you got in trouble yesterday?" Nick asked.

Brad rolled his eyes. "Mr. Hildreth found me in the bathroom playing a game."

"You shouldn't play games if you said you wouldn't," Nick said.

"If I gave you a candy bar right now, would you eat it?" Brad asked with a scowl.

"I hope not," Nick said. "Why would you do that to me?" he asked.

Brad grunted and pushed away from the wall. Nick followed him. They walked towards the playsets. The other kids were climbing the monkey bars. Some were on the swings. Some were going down the slide. Nick saw Riley acting like a monster and chasing a couple of second graders. *Probably Big Foot*, Nick thought.

Brad dropped down on an empty bench. Nick sat down next to him.

Brad shoved his hands into his coat pockets. "Don't nag me."

Riley was suddenly in front of them. "Hi, guys. What're you doing?"

"Sitting here," Brad said.

"Can I sit down?" Riley asked.

The boys shrugged.

Riley sat down. "I'm sorry I talk about Big Foot so much. My dad says

my brain locks down on things and I can't unlock it."

"Everybody does that," Nick said. "Just don't get me in trouble in class."

"I'm really sorry," Riley said again. "Please don't stop being my friends."

Nick gave him a quick look. "It's okay. We're still friends."

The three boys didn't say anything for a minute.

"What would you like to talk about?" Riley asked.

"Let's talk about *candy*," Brad said.

Nick pushed him off of the bench.

CHAPTER SEVEN

Back & Forth

The weekend slipped by with all of the things that normally kept the Perry family busy. Chores on Saturday morning. Playtime and homework in the afternoon.

Lizzy found the strength to walk downstairs. She sat in the family room for an hour or so. Then she went back to her room and slept for the rest of the day.

Mrs. Perry went to Mass on Saturday evening so she could stay with Lizzy on Sunday morning. Mr. Perry and the remaining three kids went to Mass at the normal time on Sunday.

Sam thought about hamburgers. She was aware of every hamburger restaurant they drove past. She thought she could smell hamburgers on the grill. She wished she hadn't given up hamburgers for Lent.

Nick did his best not to think about candy. It was hard. The more he tried not to think about it, the more he thought about it. Then he thought of the teasing he would get from Andrew if he ate chocolate. *I won't do it*, he told himself.

Nick's father asked him about his wrist exercises. Nick said, "They're okay."

But Nick hadn't really been doing them.

Monday came sooner than the twins wanted.

School made Sam think about the spelling bee again. She wondered what kinds of words she would have to spell.

Nick thought that Riley did better in class. He didn't talk about Big Foot when he wasn't supposed to. But Nick saw that Riley had drawn pictures of Big Foot all over his notebook.

In the back corner of the library, Nick caught Brad playing his computer game. Nick wondered out loud if Brad should go to Confession for that. Brad said, "Leave me alone" and walked away.

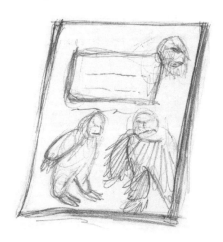

After school, Nick, Brad, and Riley walked together to the carpool area. They saw Mr. Norm moving desks in one of the classrooms.

"Let's ask," Riley said and dashed in. Nick and Brad followed him in.

"Did you talk to John Hunter?" Riley asked Mr. Norm.

Mr. Norm pushed a desk against the wall. "I saw him over the weekend. We went ice fishing."

"Will he talk to us about Big Foot?" Riley asked.

Mr. Norm nodded and said, "He said he'd let you see the Big Foot displays at his house. Come on Saturday morning. But one of your parents has to come with you."

"I'll talk to my dad," Nick said.

Nick went out to the carpool lanes. Mrs. Perry was there to pick them up. She had a surprise for Nick. It wasn't a good one.

"I'll take you home," she said. "Then I'm taking you to the doctor."

"Why?" Nick asked. He didn't like going to the doctor.

"To look at your wrist," his mom said. "Remember?"

Nick groaned.

An hour later, Nick was sitting with his mother at the doctor's office. It wasn't Nick's normal doctor. This was Dr. Sheen. He was a doctor who would help make his wrist strong again.

The doctor had Nick sit on the examination table. He held Nick's wrist in his hand and then moved it back and forth and up and down.

"Does that hurt?" Dr. Sheen asked.

Nick winced. "A little bit."

"Are you doing the exercises?" he asked.

"Sometimes," Nick said. He glanced at his mother. She gazed at him.

Dr. Sheen moved the wrist around more. "You need to do those exercises three times a day," he said.

Nick frowned. "*Three* times?" he asked.

The doctor nodded. "They're not that hard."

"Yes they are," Nick said.

The doctor chuckled, then said, "If you don't strengthen your wrist, you could hurt it again."

"Okay," Nick agreed. He hoped the doctor would let them leave.

The doctor smiled at him. "Let's do some of those exercises now."

Nick groaned. He knew he wasn't going to enjoy the exercises.

And he was right.

On the drive home, his mom said, "Do I have to watch you do those exercises or will you do them by yourself?"

"I'll do them by myself," Nick said.

"Promise?" his mom asked.

Nick made a noise that sounded like a yes, but it might not have been.

Chapter Eight

Sand & Snacks

The twins stepped onto the yellow school bus. It was early Wednesday morning and the third grade was going to the Great Sand Dunes of Colorado. They were told to bundle up in winter clothes and boots. The dunes were a three-hour ride from Hope Springs.

Father Cliff went with them. He sat on the front seat behind the driver. He brought his guitar and led the kids in a couple of songs.

Sister Lucy moved up and down the aisle. She had a whistle around her neck. "If I blow this, then you should stop talking. If I blow it at the dunes, then you need to come running."

She used some of the time on the bus to explain about the dunes.

"The Great Sand Dunes are near the Sangre de Cristo mountains," she said. "Sangre de Cristo means 'the blood of Christ.' A Spanish explorer named Antonio Valverde y Cosio called them that because of how red the mountains looked at sunrise."

Some of the kids chuckled. Sam thought how the word "Colorado" meant "red," too.

Sister Lucy continued, "The dunes are the tallest in North America. The High Dune goes up to 650 feet. The Star Dune reaches 750 feet. We have to walk across the Medano Creek to get to the dunes. It's frozen now, but we had you wear your boots just in case."

They reached the sand dunes late

in the morning. Sam thought it was strange to see a giant desert with snow-covered mountains behind it.

The bus pulled into a parking lot in front of a long brown building. That was the visitor center. The kids went inside and looked at displays, videos, paintings, and photos about the dunes.

They got back on the bus and drove to a parking lot closer to the dunes. From there, the dunes looked like a light brown mountain range. Sister Lucy told them all to hold hands and led them across the frozen Medano Creek. On the other side was the start of the dunes. The sand stretched far and wide and then rose up into hills that went higher and higher.

There was a light cold wind that blew steadily, then it sometimes hit them in blasts.

"Stay where you can see me or Father Cliff or the other parents," Sister Lucy shouted. "If you can't see us, then you are in the wrong place. If I blow the whistle, come right away."

Sam saw Nick and Brad run to the first dune. Riley was close behind them.

"Do you want to run to the top?" Sam asked Kim.

Kim stood where she was. She shivered. "No, thanks," she said unhappily. "I thought the desert was supposed to be *warm*."

Nick, Brad, and Riley had reached the top of the dune. They pointed at something in the distance. Then Nick turned and waved at Sam. He wanted her to come up to the top.

"Go without me," Kim said.

Sam ran to the dune. It was harder than she thought to get to the top. The sand was hard, but her boots sunk just enough to need more effort. She was panting by the time she got to the top.

"Look that way," Nick said to her.

The sand dunes looked like an ocean of giant tan waves. She had never seen anything like it.

A gust of wind peppered her face with sand. She closed her eyes and turned away.

"Do you think we can ski down the dune?" Brad shouted.

"You go first," Nick suggested.

"I'll go!" Riley said and then jumped. He made it a few feet but his boots landed solidly in the sand.

"Ha," said Brad.

Riley tried again. He jumped downward. This time his boots stopped in the sand, but Riley's upper body kept going. He tumbled onward, bouncing and rolling. Near the bottom he stopped again and rolled over onto his back.

"That was *great!*" he shouted.

Nick and Brad looked at each other.

Sam knew what they were thinking.

Both boys dove at the sand. They

bounced, flipped, and spun to the bottom.

Sam carefully walked down after them.

Father Cliff stood at the bottom of the dune. He looked at the three boys, who were lying on their backs and laughing. Sam walked up to him.

He was smiling when he said to the boys, "You're covered with sand. Did you bring a change of clothes?"

"No," Nick said. The boys looked at each other. They hadn't thought through how it would feel to spend the rest of the day with sand all over them.

The boys stood up. They dusted themselves off.

Sam watched the three boys twitch and shake. The sand was already working its way to their skin.

"Do you know what that's called?" Father Cliff asked.

"No," Nick said quietly.

"Consequences," Father Cliff said.

There were trails near the dunes that led into a raw forest of pines and brown grass and eroded earth. Mule deer grazed in a clearing nearby.

"We came here to help us think about Jesus and his forty days in the desert," Father Cliff said as he led them along. "Imagine walking through the desert by yourself for forty days. No food. Little shelter."

Sam thought about it. *No food for forty days?* She had a hard time picturing it.

Father Cliff continued, "Jesus went into the desert to clear away all the distractions. There were no televisions, cell phones, video games, family, or friends to take his mind off of God. I'm pretty sure some of you think giving up those things would be harder than giving up food."

Some of the kids laughed.

"Lent is like journeying into the desert alone. We give up the things that distract," Father Cliff said. "And guess what? The devil tempts us when we're alone. He tempts us when we're trying to pray. He tempts us to forget that we are baptized children of God. Do you remember how Satan tempted Jesus?"

A girl named Jayden raised her hand. "He told Jesus to turn the stones into bread," she said.

"That's right," Father Cliff said. "Jesus must have been very hungry by this time. So Satan said that *if* Jesus was the Son of God, then he should turn these rocks into bread. He was testing who Jesus was. It's a nasty trick. *If* you are the Son of God *you'll do it.* If you *don't do it* then you're not

really the Son of God. But Jesus saw the trick. Jesus knew how the devil likes to use our desire against us. He tempts us with things we really want. He uses all kinds of tricks to distract us. But Jesus used the Bible to put the devil in his place."

They walked on. Sam looked out at the ragged trees, the tufts of grass and the dry rivers of dirt.

"How else did Satan tempt Jesus?" asked Father Cliff.

The kids had more trouble with this one.

Sister Lucy said, "He took Jesus to the top of the temple. He said to Jesus, 'If you are the Son of God, then throw yourself off and the angels will save you.'"

Father Cliff said, "Thank you, Sister. Do you see what Satan did this time? He wanted Jesus to prove who he was by jumping from that building. Jesus hit Satan with another verse from the

Bible. 'You shall not tempt the Lord your God.' So, what was the third temptation?"

"I'll give you everything," Sam said.

Father Cliff turned to Sam. "Say that again, please."

Sam spoke louder this time. "Satan said that if Jesus would bow down and worship him, he would give Jesus everything."

"That's right. He would give Jesus all of the kingdoms and glory of the world," Father Cliff said. "What did Jesus say?"

"He used another Bible verse," Kim said. She walked next to Sam. "He said we're only supposed to worship and serve the Lord God."

Father Cliff smiled at her. "Very good. Let's think about that. Jesus had been in the desert for forty days. He was hungry, alone, and tired. To be fed, to be saved by the angels, to be given great power must have sounded pretty good then. But Jesus said no to all of it."

A bird called out overhead. Sam looked up and watched it soar past.

"Jesus knew who he was—the Son of God," Father Cliff said. "He knew what he was here to do—to save us from our sins. So I have to ask: who are you and what are you here to do?"

"We're children of God," said a boy named Dave.

"Why are we here?" Father Cliff asked.

"To love and serve God," said a girl named Karen.

"That's right," said Father Cliff. "Lent is a time to remember that. Lent is when we say a clear 'yes' to God and 'no' to Satan."

On the way back to Hope Springs,

the bus stopped at a diner and grocery store on the side of the road. The bus driver—a man named Arthur—said it served the best hamburgers in Colorado.

"Hamburgers?" Sam whimpered to Kim. "Why does it have to be hamburgers?"

Kim laughed. "You'll know better next Lent."

Sister Lucy stood up and said, "If you brought your lunch, eat it here. Or you can buy something to eat."

Many of the kids clambered off the bus.

Nick was sitting behind Sam. He had been complaining the whole drive about how itchy the sand was. Now he said, "I forgot my lunch."

Sam looked at Kim. Kim rolled her eyes.

Nick leaned forward. "Sam, do you have any money?"

"No," Sam said. "But you can have some of my lunch."

"What is it?" he asked.

Sam took her lunch bag out of her backpack. "Mom packed some veggies, a peanut butter and jelly sandwich, and some crackers."

"Can I have the crackers?" Nick asked. Sam handed him the bag.

"Thank you," he said.

Sam could hear him tear open the small paper bag.

Then Sam heard Brad say, "I have a protein bar. It's healthy."

Nick said, "That's chocolate."

"But it's good for you," Brad said. "You can have it if you want."

Sam realized that Brad was teasing Nick. She waited to see what Nick would do.

"Man does not live by chocolate alone," Nick said.

Sam smiled.

"I'll eat that protein bar if you don't want it," Riley said.

"Go buy your own," snapped Brad.

Poor Riley, Sam thought. She turned in her seat. "Riley, you can have half of my sandwich." She passed it back to him.

"Thanks!" he said.

Brad made a face at her. "*Saint* Sam."

Sam turned to face front again. "That would be nice," she said.

The trip to the Great Sand Dunes helped Sam forget all about the spelling bee. She didn't think about it when the bus returned to the school. It wasn't on her mind when her mom drove them home. But it came back to her fast when she opened her backpack in her room. On top of her books was a folded piece of paper. It looked just like the one she'd torn up.

On one of the folds were the handwritten words: Help for the next round.

"Oh no," she whispered. She unfolded the paper.

It was the list of words she had to study. Ten of the words were circled.

She crumpled the paper up and held it in her fist.

She struggled. She wanted to look at the words. It would help to know what they were. But she knew that would be cheating.

She moved the paper from one fist to the other.

A quick peek wouldn't be so bad, she thought.

She looked at the ball of paper in her hand.

God, help me, she prayed.

Then she tore up the paper into little pieces and dropped it into the trash can.

She slumped into her desk chair.

Who is trying to help me? she wondered. *And how do I make whoever-it-is stop?*

CHAPTER NINE

Saints & Spellers

Friday arrived, along with Saint Patrick. His feast day was the next Sunday.

He stood on the stage in the assembly hall. He had wild white hair and a beard. He was dressed in a green tunic that covered his body. A belt that looked like a gold rope was tied in a knot around his waist. A brown cape draped his shoulders. He held onto a tall wooden shepherd's crook.

Nick thought his voice sounded a lot like Deacon Chuck doing an Irish accent.

He pounded his crook against the stage floor and said, "Good morning to you! Patrick, I am. 'Tis a pleasure to be invited by the good sisters here to talk to you."

Some of the audience chuckled.

Nick heard a child behind him whisper, "Is that Santa Claus?"

"Shall we find out how much you know about me?" Saint Patrick asked. "Can anyone tell me in what century I was born?"

No one spoke. Finally, an adult raised her hand and said, "Late in the fourth century?"

"Aye," he said. "They say I was born in three hundred and eighty-five, though I was too young to remember it for myself."

A few people laughed.

"Where was I born?" he asked.

Several voices called out, "Ireland!"

Saint Patrick chuckled, then said, "Well now, that's where you'd be wrong. I was born in what you now call Britain. But, when I was a lad, some pirates kidnapped me and took me to Ireland as a slave."

A few of the kids gasped.

"For seven years I lived in the wilds of that pagan country, tending the sheep, braving the worst possible weather," Saint Patrick said. "But God did it to knock some sense into me. I was a stubborn young man, you see, and turned away from the faith of my parents. I thought I knew better than everyone. I didn't believe in God or his Son or his word. Let me tell you: seven years as a slave in the wild will show you how foolish you can be. I learned a lot about God and his mercy."

He moved across the stage, tapping his crook on the floor as he went. Then he walked down the stairs and walked along the aisle.

He said, "God rescued me from slavery and let me go home again. It wasn't easy. I knew my life had changed. I couldn't go back to what I was. Do you know why?"

A seventh grader raised her hand and said, "God told you to go back to Ireland."

Saint Patrick pointed to the girl and said, "He did indeed! 'Twas the very thing he told me to do. Why would he ask me to do such a thing?" he asked.

Another hand went up. A fifth-grade boy said, "To make them see the truth."

"What smart children you have here!" Saint Patrick said. "The people of Ireland worshipped false and evil gods. They did terrible things to their own people. And God told me to go back and tell them about Jesus and his Church."

He paused and looked at the audience.

"What would you say if God asked you to do such a thing?" he asked.

The audience shuffled in their seats.

"Some of you might say, 'No! That's asking too much!'" He banged his crook against the floor. "But you remember what happened to Jonah when he said 'no' to God. He got swallowed by a big fish! You wouldn't want to be swallowed by a big fish, I don't think."

Soft laughter rolled through the crowd.

"The truth of it is that I couldn't say no to God. In my heart, I knew I had to go back. Even if they killed me, I had to go back. The people needed to hear the Truth and God told me to take it to them. So I did."

He gazed at the audience for a moment.

"What then?" he asked. "What

became of me?"

A young girl raised her hand. "You drove the snakes out of Ireland," she said in a squeaky voice.

Saint Patrick smiled. "There are a lot of stories about me and snakes and three-leaf clovers. Can you think of something I did with fire?"

It took a moment, but then one of the parents said, "You lit a giant bonfire to show everyone God's power."

"Aye!" Saint Patrick said. "On a night when the pagans planned to light a fire to their gods, I lit a bigger *paschal* fire to the one true God. They weren't happy about that. But it showed the people that I was ready to do *anything* to tell them about the truth of Jesus."

Saint Patrick walked back onto the stage. "I spent my life teaching and preaching in Ireland. The people there gave up the false Gods and turned to Jesus and his Church."

He leaned on his crook, then said, "Lent is a good time to ask yourself: what is God calling *me* to do?"

Saint Patrick walked off the stage behind the curtain.

A few people applauded. Then a few more. Then everyone joined in.

Nick thought about the question. *What is God calling me to do?*

The kids assembled onstage again for the spelling bee. Sister Stephanie explained the rules for everyone and then they began. The two first graders spelled their words. The second grader already had a winner from last time, so Sister Stephanie asked Sam and Karl to go to the microphones.

Nick watched Sam. He knew she was nervous. She had twisted up the bottom of her sweater.

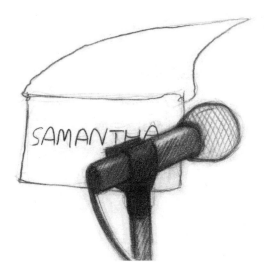

Sister Stephanie went back and forth between the two kids. Sam's words were "Finish," "Myself," "Holy," "Shepherd," and, finally, "Filet."

Nick closed his eyes on that word. It was a hard one. *Did it have two L's in the middle? Was it "a-y" at the end?*

Sam paused. The silence filled the room. Karl looked at her.

Then she slowly said, "F-I-L" – she paused again and then resumed, "L-E-T."

Sister Stephanie leaned into her microphone. "You stopped in the middle so I'm not sure if you spelled it with one 'L' or two. Please spell it again."

Sam said slowly, "F-I-L-E-T."

"That is correct," Sister Stephanie said.

Nick's mom and a few other people applauded.

Karl's last word was "Purple." He spelled it correctly and the two of them sat down.

Nick saw Sam take a deep breath. She slumped down a little as if she were tired. Karl looked at the audience with a big grin on his face.

Sam decided after the spelling bee to tell Sister Lucy about the notes. She waited until everyone left the classroom for music practice to talk to her.

Sister Lucy listened carefully. She looked bothered. "Did you *read* the words?" she asked.

"No," Sam said. "The first time I saw that the words were circled but didn't look closely at them. The second time I crumpled it up before I could see the words."

"Do you have the notes with you?" Sister Lucy asked.

Sam shook her head. "I tore them up and threw them away."

"If it happens again, don't unfold the note. Give it to me if you're here at school. Give it to one of your parents if you're at home. Tell them to bring it to me. I might know the handwriting."

"Okay," Sam said.

"You *promise* you didn't read the words?" her teacher asked. "I'd be tempted to look."

"I promise. I was tempted, but I didn't do it," Sam said.

"I'm proud of you," Sister Lucy said.

The family had fish for dinner that night.

Nick's father agreed to take the boys to John Hunter's house the next day. Andrew wanted to go, but had promised to meet a friend in town at that time.

Lizzy came down from her room to sit with them. Nick thought she looked pale. Her pajamas hung on her like they were two sizes too big. Her eyes were red. She ran her fingers through the matted hair on her head. She smiled, but it seemed to take a lot of work for her to do it.

"How are you feeling?" her father asked.

Lizzy gave a small shrug of her shoulders. "All I want to do is sleep."

"That's what your body needs," her father said.

Her mother pressed a hand to her forehead. "I think your fever is gone."

"It goes away and then comes back again," Lizzy said.

Her mother got up and made soup for her. Lizzy moved the spoon around, but Nick didn't see her eat any. Finally Lizzy nibbled on a saltine cracker.

Sam told them about the mystery of the spelling bee list.

Mr. Perry asked, "Who would want to help you like that?"

"I don't know," said Sam.

Mrs. Perry looked concerned. "If another list shows up, tell Sister Lucy or bring it to me."

Sam agreed.

The family helped clear the dishes from the table. Nick picked up a plate in his right hand and a bowl with his left. He almost dropped the bowl.

Nick's father saw it. "Are you doing your wrist exercises?" he asked.

Nick tried to sound like he had, even though he hadn't.

"Was that a yes or a no?" his dad asked. He looked Nick in the eyes.

"Sort of," Nick admitted. "But not really."

Nick's mom sighed loudly.

"Go get the sheet. We'll watch you do them now," his dad said.

"But I have homework to do," Nick countered.

"You'll have plenty of time for homework after you do the exercises," his dad said.

"But I don't like the exercises," Nick complained.

His dad folded his arms. "Nick, it's not about liking them or not. Your wrist won't get stronger if you don't do the exercises. It's that simple. Go get the sheet."

Nick pouted. "Yes, sir."

Nick ran up to his room. He thought about losing the sheet somewhere in his various papers and clutter.

But he knew his parents would make him search until he found it again.

Then he thought that it would be *too late* to do any exercises.

"No stalling," his dad said from the doorway.

"Aw," Nick whined.

The exercises were just as hard as he thought they would be.

CHAPTER TEN

Prancers & Perrys

On Saturday, Nick and his father drove to John Hunter's house. It sat down a short street that had only two other houses on it. The street didn't look like it had been repaved for decades. Drifts of old snow lined one side of the road. Mr. Perry had to drive carefully around the potholes.

John Hunter's house was at the dead end of the street. It was nestled into a small hill with a patch of woods behind it. A little driveway led to a double garage. The house sat on top of the garage. A staircase to the right of the garage led far up to the front door of the house. Nick counted the steps. There were twenty-four.

Nick's dad rang the doorbell. From somewhere inside came a loud "roar."

"Was that a gorilla?" Nick asked with wide eyes.

"I'll bet it's a recording of Big Foot," Mr. Perry said.

The door opened. A man with dark wrinkled skin stood in front of them. He looked at them with deep brown eyes. He had straight white hair with a braid that curled over his right shoulder. The braid had different colored beads in them. He wore a brown top that might have been made of buckskin and black pants that dropped into knee-high leather boots.

"Welcome, Jon," the man said. He stretched out his hand to Mr. Perry.

Mr. Perry shook his hand. "Thanks for allowing us to come over."

"And you, Nick." He put out his hand and Nick shook it. "It is good to have more Perrys back in Hope Springs. I have always considered your family my friends."

"We feel the same, Mr. Hunter," Mr. Perry said.

"Why so formal?" he asked. "When you were small, you called me Prancer."

"I did?" Mr. Perry looked surprised.

John Hunter nodded. "When you first learned to talk. Your grandfather and father brought you to see me from time to time. We would sit around the potbelly stove and talk for as long as you would let us."

Mr. Perry's face lit up as if the memory had just come back to him. "You played checkers on an old wooden table," he said.

John Hunter smiled.

"What should the kids call you?" Mr. Perry asked.

"They may call me Elder Jack," he replied.

Nick and his dad walked into a small hall that quickly opened into a larger living room. It had three large chairs and a sofa circling a pot-belly stove. A tall hutch with plates and cups sat along the wall. A small TV was tucked in the corner next to a wooden table and chairs. The walls were made of wood panels. Dark red curtains hung on each side of the front window. Nick could see a kitchen through a doorway in the middle of the back wall.

Brad and Riley were sitting on the sofa. They stood up as soon as they saw Nick.

"Hey," they said.

Nick gave a small wave.

"Elder Jack has been telling us about the 'Ye'iitsoh,'" Riley said, speaking the last word carefully.

" 'Ye'iitsoh' is the Navajo word for Big Foot," Elder Jack explained. "Follow me."

Elder Jack opened a nearby door and headed down a long staircase.

The boys followed him. Mr. Perry followed the boys.

The stairs were wooden. They creaked and groaned.

Nick heard Brad and then Riley gasp. He did the same when he saw the giant room at the bottom of the stairs.

"This is my collection," Elder Jack said.

The room was filled with glass displays, large photos, newspaper clippings, and maps hanging on the wall. Everyone spread out into the room.

Nick looked at the glass cases first. Inside were gigantic bones and casts of very large feet, handprints, and sculptures of huge heads. The heads were covered with hair and had faces with narrow eyes, wide noses, and open mouths with jagged teeth.

Nick noticed that the feet had four toes together on one side and a large toe sticking away from the other four.

A small TV on a table showed a film from 1967 of a Big Foot walking along a creek. That was followed by other film clips of a Big Foot behind branches, in the snow, on a distant cliff, and peeking from behind a tree.

The maps on the wall had stars where a Big Foot had been seen in parts of the world. Little tags also noted the dates.

The newspaper articles were all about people who had claimed to see Big Foot.

Riley pointed to different parts of the displays and asked Elder Jack question after question.

"Where did you see Big Foot?" Nick asked Elder Jack.

"Up at the Little Big Pond," he said. "I think they live near there," Elder Jack added.

"*They?*" Riley asked.

"I believe there's a family of them," Elder Jack said. "It's hard to tell because they move around in different seasons."

Nick's dad was standing next to a model of a Big Foot. "Did you really see your first one when you were a kid?"

Elder Jack said, "I was Nick's age. I heard my father talking to a man about the Sasquatch at the Little Big Pond. The man said he had seen one there.

I went with my father and the man to see for myself. There it was—plain as day. I saw it. We all did."

"Who was the other man?" Mr. Perry asked.

Elder Jack gave him a sly smile. "Your great-grandfather."

Mr. Perry's mouth fell open.

"My ancestor saw Big Foot?" Nick asked.

"Yes. Theodore Perry himself," Elder Jack said with a laugh.

"You're so lucky!" Riley cried out.

Brad gazed at him. "You're a star."

"I never heard that story," Nick's dad said.

"I'm sure there are a lot of stories you never heard in your family," Elder Jack said. "Theodore Perry kept a lot of things to himself."

Nick tried to imagine how the man standing in front of him knew his great-

great-grandfather. He asked. "How old are you?"

Elder Jack patted Nick on the head. "Old enough to know better than to answer that question."

Nick and his friends looked at the displays for almost an hour. Nick's dad and Elder Jack went back upstairs to drink coffee and talk. Once or twice Nick heard them laughing.

"We have to go to the Little Big Pond," Riley said.

"That's a long way to see nothing," Brad said.

"Nothing!" Riley cried out.

Brad scowled. "You don't really believe this stuff."

Riley waved his arms around and said, "Aren't you looking? Can't you see all the proof?"

Brad snorted.

"Don't worry about him," Nick

said to Riley. "Brad doesn't believe in anything."

Nick's dad called out from upstairs, "Come on, boys. It's time to go."

Riley glared at Brad, then marched up the steps.

"Do you believe it?" Brad asked Nick.

Nick shrugged. "I don't know."

The two went up the steps. By the time they got there, Riley was already asking if Elder Jack would take them all to the Little Big Pond.

"I will take you," Elder Jack said. "If your parents agree."

Nick looked at his father.

Mr. Perry thought for a moment. "I'd like to tag along myself."

Nick smiled.

"We'll go on a Saturday," Elder Jack said.

"*Next* Saturday?" Riley asked.

"The Saturday before Palm Sunday,"

Elder Jack said. "We can meet at the Pine Creek Pass building site at nine in the morning."

CHAPTER ELEVEN

Soup & Surprises

St. Clare of Assisi Catholic Church ran a soup kitchen and food pantry in an old building a block away from the town's main street. Nick heard Andrew tell his mother that the building was originally a clothing warehouse in the 1920s. It was left to ruin when the Depression hit in the 1930s. St. Clare's bought the building after World War II and used it for classes until the newer school was built in the 1970s. People came there when they had lost their jobs or couldn't feed their children or pay their rent.

Volunteers from the church and the town served meals or passed out bags of food to whoever needed them. There were rooms on the upper floors for families that didn't have a place to live.

Nick wondered how Andrew knew so much about the town's history.

It was Tuesday evening. Mrs. Perry took Nick, Sam, and Andrew to the soup kitchen to help out. It was one of their Lenten promises. Andrew was told to keep the water glasses filled on the tables. He spent the night carrying a big silver pitcher around. Nick and Sam were given the job of picking up any dirty dishes and wiping the tables.

Nick was surprised by how many people came. He counted over one hundred during the main dinner time. He thought everyone would look and dress like homeless people living on the street. Some of the guests wore nice clothing. Some were older, some were the same age as Nick's parents and had kids Nick's age. Some had babies in strollers.

Nick pushed a gray cart over to a table to collect the dishes. He suddenly stopped short. Riley was sitting at a corner table. He was in his school uniform, finishing a plate of food.

"What are you doing here?" Nick asked him.

Riley went bug-eyed when he saw Nick. He nearly choked on his food. "I ... came to help."

"By eating?" Nick asked.

"I was washing the dishes in the back," he said quickly. "They let me have dinner."

A man in grease-stained tanned overalls walked up to them. He had red hair that stuck out in different places. He hunched a little, like he carried something heavy on his shoulders.

"We need you in the stock room." He spoke with a slow drawl.

"Okay," Riley said. He wiped his mouth on a napkin and stood up.

The man glanced at Nick, then said, "Who's your friend?"

"He's from school," Riley said.

The man looked like he expected Riley to introduce them.

Riley didn't. He walked past both of them and headed for the back.

The man nodded to Nick, then walked off.

That was weird, Nick thought.

Sam came up alongside of him. "Did you see Riley?" she asked.

"He said he's helping out," Nick said.

"Is that all?" she asked.

"What else would he be doing?" Nick asked.

"I don't know," she said and picked up a stack of dirty plates.

As the night went on, Nick picked up a lot of dishes. He had to flex his left wrist to keep it from aching.

"Is your wrist all right?" his mom asked him as they drove home.

"It's okay," he said. It wasn't, but he was afraid she would make him do more exercises.

She looked in the rearview mirror. "Did you enjoy helping out at the soup kitchen?" she asked all three of them.

The kids agreed that they did.

"I'll volunteer for more time," Mrs. Perry said. "They need the help."

Nick thought about Riley and the man in the overalls.

The next day at school Nick asked Riley about the soup kitchen. Riley blushed a little. "I was helping out."

Nick asked, "Who was the man—?"

Riley cut him off. "I don't want to talk about it." He turned away and acted like he was reading a book.

Nick noticed that the book was upside down.

Sam was distracted. She watched her classmates every time one of them went to the coat closet. If one came near her or her backpack, she tensed up. She looked at her friends and wondered which one might want to help her.

Sister Lucy gave her the big list of words. Another *one hundred*. She glanced them over and saw that some were words she'd been given before.

Kim looked at the list at lunch while Sam practiced the spellings. She crossed off the ones Sam knew well.

Over *seventy* words were left. Some of those were very hard.

At home, Sam went to her room to do homework. She opened her math book. A folded piece of paper was tucked inside. She groaned and took it out.

This time she resisted the temptation to look by taking it straight to her mother.

Mrs. Perry unfolded the paper. "It's the list," she said. "It looks like ten words were circled."

"Is there a handwritten note?" Sam asked.

Mrs. Perry checked both sides of the paper. "Not this time. We'll take it to Sister Lucy tomorrow."

Sister Lucy looked at the folded piece of paper first thing in the morning. "That's too bad. I had hoped to use the handwriting to figure out who is doing this."

"How are they sneaking it in without me seeing?" Sam asked. "I keep my backpack with me all the time now."

Sister Lucy folded the paper up again and dropped it on her desk. "You said it was tucked in your math book?"

"Yes," Sam said.

"Who was near you the last time you had your math book out?" she asked.

Sam tried, but couldn't remember.

Mrs. Perry stood next to the desk. She asked, "How would one of your students know which words are going to be used?"

"That's a very good question," Sister Lucy said. "I'll try to find out."

The third round of the spelling bee was Friday morning, as usual. The number of contestants thinned out as kids misspelled words, leaving one winner for each class. Sam and Karl were still tied. Sam's words were "Forty," "Prayer," "Thumb," "Psalm," and "Penitence."

The last word was difficult for her. She couldn't remember if it ended in 'ence' or 'ance." She guessed and got it right.

"Why don't they have rules about it?" she asked Sister Lucy after it was over.

Sister Lucy explained, "English has grown and changed for the last several hundred years. Many of our spellings aren't consistent."

Sam thought about the word "consistent," then smiled and asked, "Is that spelled with an 'ant' or 'ent'?"

Chapter Twelve

Changes & Chats

It was during the fourth week of Lent that Nick realized something had changed. Brad seemed to sneak off at every recess to play on his game device. Riley talked about the latest Big Foot news but wouldn't talk about anything else. If Nick asked him about what he did after school, he always said, "It's nothing special." If Nick asked him what other things he was interested in, he always said, "Nothing special." If Nick asked him about his family or his life at home, he always said, "It's nothing special."

Nick also noticed that Riley walked toward town at the end of the school day.

"Do you ever wonder about Riley?" Nick asked Brad one day.

"No," Brad replied.

"He never talks about his parents or if he has brothers or sisters," Nick said.

"So?" Brad said. "I don't like to talk about my parents or brother or sister. You don't talk about your family very much."

Nick had to think about that.

Brad reached into his pocket. He took out a chocolate bar. "Oh, look!" he said as if it was a big surprise. "I have some candy."

Nick rolled his eyes.

Brad waved the candy bar in front of Nick. "It's been a *long* time since you had one."

Nick pushed the chocolate away. "Don't do this to me," he said.

"Do what?" Brad asked. He slowly tore at the wrapper and put the bar to his mouth for a big bite.

"You're not a very good friend," Nick said and walked away.

This time Sam found the folded spelling bee list shoved in her coat pocket. It fell out when she pulled out her mittens at recess. She gave the paper to Sister Lucy. There was nothing on the paper to give away who had put it in coat.

Sam looked over the official list with Kim.

"It's a nasty trick," Sam said.

Many of the words were connected to food. She saw "Bun" and "Ketchup"

and "Mustard" and "Pickle" and even "*Hamburger.*"

"It's not fair," Sam said.

Kim laughed. Then she pointed to the page. "Look, there's 'ramen.'"

The two girls talked about how *everything* seemed to remind them of the thing they'd given up for Lent.

They wondered why that was.

"I blame Adam and Eve," Kim said.

The week ended with the fourth spelling bee round.

Sam had to spell "Heavy" and "Scratch" and "Point" and "Raised" and "Buses." She nearly spelled "buses" with two "s"es in the middle but stopped herself before she did.

Karl spelled all of his words correctly.

By the end of the event, there were only ten contestants left.

Students from the two third-grade classes began to talk about who would finally win. It was like two football teams, with fans rooting for "Team Karl" or "Team Sam."

Sam thought it was funny. But she also felt a new kind of pressure. Before she wanted to win so Sister Lucy would be proud. Now she needed to win so she wouldn't let her classmates down.

CHAPTER THIRTEEN

Taunts & Ties

Lizzy felt well enough to go back to school during the fifth week of Lent. Sam thought her sister looked normal on Monday. On Tuesday, she seemed tired again. By Wednesday, she had to stay home again.

"Relapse" was the word the doctor used. Lizzy needed to stay home until after the Easter break.

"Relapse" was also on the list of spelling bee words.

Sam watched for the folded piece of

paper to appear somewhere. Wednesday came and went. No sign of the circled words.

The next day she opened her lunch box. The folded piece of paper was tucked inside next to a bag of potato chips.

She almost closed the lid so Kim wouldn't see it. She told herself that she wanted to take it home to her mom. She then told herself that she really wanted to sneak a peek at it because she was worried about losing the contest.

Sam took a deep breath and said a simple prayer: *help.*

She opened the lid again and put the folded paper on the table in front of Kim.

Kim's mouth fell open. "How did it get in *there*?" she asked.

Sam shrugged.

Kim opened the list. "No handwriting," she said.

Sister Lucy was lunch monitor that day. Sam gave her the list.

"I have an idea about who is doing this," Sister Lucy said as she tucked the list into her pocket.

"Who?" Sam asked.

Sister Lucy gave her a little smile. "I can't say until I know for sure."

On the way back to class, Sam bumped into Karl in the hall.

"You're spelling better than I thought," Karl said.

Sam said, "Everyone knew you'd do well."

He smirked at her. "Are you getting help?" he asked.

Sam frowned back at him and snapped, "Why do you ask that?"

He flinched with surprise. "Just asking. You don't have to get mad about it."

Sam went into her class. She sat down at her desk.

"What's wrong?" Nick asked.

"Nothing." She folded her arms and pressed her lips together.

Riley leaned from his desk onto Nick's. "Hey Sam—are you going to the Little Big Pond with us on Saturday?"

Sam shot him a glance. "No, thank you."

"It'll be fun," Riley said.

"I'll be hiding in my room," she said.

"Why?" askcd Riley.

"Because I'll lose the spelling bcc contest and never want to show my face again," Sam said.

Nick looked at his sister. "Don't take it so serious," Nick said.

"Serious-*ly*," Sam said to him. "S-E-R-I-O-" she stopped herself. She didn't know how to spell the word. "Never mind," she growled.

Nick sat back in his chair. *Is everybody having a nervous breakdown?*

He turned to Riley.

Riley held up a color picture of Big Foot. "Saturday's the big day."

Sam's sweater was all twisted up by the time she stepped up to the microphone on Friday. This was the next-to-last spelling bee. She had studied the words all evening. She dreamed about them. She woke up thinking about them.

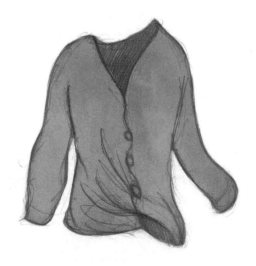

Then Sister Stephanie gave her the words.

"Famish."

"Delicate."

"Irritate."

"Sacrifice."

"Reconcile."

Sam nearly blew it with three of the words. She had to ask Sister Stephanie to use the words in sentences.

She heard the kids in the audience groan each time.

Some of them cheered loudly for Karl. He spelled his words without any trouble.

At the end, there were only six contestants left.

Sam was one of them.

"I wish I had lost," she said to Kim as they walked to class.

"Why?" Kim asked.

"Because I know I'll lose next time," Sam said. "I may as well get it over with."

CHAPTER FOURTEEN

Frights & Ice

The Saturday morning sky was thick with clouds. Nick sat in the back seat of his dad's SUV. Riley sat next to him. The boys had on their heaviest coats for their hike to find Big Foot.

Nick noticed earlier that Riley wasn't wearing his school uniform. It was the first time he'd seen Riley in normal clothes. He wore jeans and a sweater that didn't fit him very well. *Hand me downs*, he thought.

The car bumped hard as Nick's dad turned off of the main highway and onto a dirt road. He was driving them to a building site. A large sign said, "Perry Construction: The Future Home of the Pine Creek Pass Resort."

"Why is your name on the sign?" Riley asked Nick.

"My Uncle Clark is building a big hotel here. It will have skiing and fishing and all kinds of fun things for people to do."

"Is he rich?" Riley asked.

Nick sometimes wondered the same thing. "Dad, is Uncle Clark rich?"

"Your Uncle Clark is good with money," his dad said from the driver's seat.

"Are *we* rich?" Nick asked.

"We have more money than some people," his dad said. "But not as much as other people."

Nick knew that was his father's way of not answering his question.

"Maybe they can do tours to see Big

Foot," Riley said.

Mr. Perry laughed. "That's a good idea."

Nick thought about Brad. He wished his friend had come along. But Brad's last words on the subject were, "It's a waste of time. You and Linus have fun looking for the Great Pumpkin without me."

They drove up to a tall wire fence with a wide gate. A man in a uniform stepped out of a small hut. He leaned down and looked in. "Hi, Mr. Perry."

Mr. Perry put down his window. "Hi, Raylan. I'm meeting John Hunter."

The man called Raylan looked at a device in his hand. "He's here," Raylan said. "Go on up to the main office."

Raylan pushed a button on the device. The gates slowly opened.

The main office for the building site was a large trailer. It sat off to the side of a giant building that would become the hotel. Two smaller buildings stretched out to the left and right from the giant one. Steam rose from the hot springs behind the building on the right. Hope Springs had several hot springs.

Bright yellow trucks and cranes and bulldozers and dump trucks moved in different directions. Workers in bright orange hard hats and overalls were dotted everywhere.

Mr. Perry parked in front of the trailer.

"This is *huge*," Riley said as he got out of the SUV. Nick felt the cold blast of the day against his cheeks. He was glad he wore his boots, hat, and gloves.

Nick's Uncle Clark stepped through the door of the office. He walked down the wooden stairs toward them.

He went to Nick first and pulled him close for a hug. "Hey, Nick," he said warmly. Then he shook his brother's hand. "Hunting for Big Foot?" he asked.

Jon Perry smiled. "Any sight of him?"

"One of the workers saw him last week," Uncle Clark said.

Riley gasped. "Really?"

Uncle Clark leaned down to face Riley. "Really," he said. He shook Riley's hand. "You're Riley, the expert, right?"

"Right," Riley said.

Uncle Clark patted him on the shoulder. "Good to meet you."

"Have *you* ever seen Big Foot?" Riley asked.

"No. I'm never in the right place at the right time, I guess," Uncle Clark said.

"Where's Elder Jack? The guard said he's here," Nick's dad said.

"He drove his truck up the back service road," Uncle Clark said. "It's on the other side of the building site. Just follow the fence. He should be at the gate."

"Let's go," Nick's dad said.

Uncle Clark put a hand on his brother's arm. "Can we talk first?" he asked.

"Is something wrong?" Nick's dad asked.

"Just some family business." The two men moved a few steps from the boys. Uncle Clark leaned close and spoke quietly to Nick's dad.

His dad nodded. Then he looked over at Nick and said, "You guys go on ahead to the gate. I'll be along in a few minutes."

Nick and Riley walked through the construction site. They reached the trail. A hand-painted sign with an arrow pointed to the Little Big Pond.

The boys followed the path around the building site. They reached the fence that circled the property. Further along they found the open gate. There was no sign of Elder Jack.

"Maybe he drove on ahead," Riley said.

Nick looked back. His dad and uncle must still be talking.

"I know the way," Nick said. "Let's keep walking. My dad will catch up."

The service road was little more than a wide trail. The tracks had large patches of snow, like Uncle Clark said. The woods were thick with pine trees on both sides. Riley kept turning his head one way and then another.

"What's wrong?" Nick asked.

"I'm looking for Big Foot," Riley said.

"I don't think he'll step out and say hi," Nick said.

There was a loud *whoomf* off to the left. Nick jumped. A clump of snow had fallen from a branch.

The trail was mostly uphill. Nick didn't know how far they had walked from the building site. His legs ached. They rounded a bend and the view ahead opened up to a large meadow. The Little Big Pond sat in the middle of the meadow. It was covered with ice and snow.

"It's gigantic!" Riley said. He went from a walk to a run.

Nick followed. He wondered where Elder Jack was. He hoped they were on the right side of the lake. He didn't want to walk all the way around.

They reached the edge of the lake. A large sign said *Danger!* and *Keep Off the Ice* and had a long list of rules about swimming and starting fires and picnics and fishing. Nick didn't read them all.

The two boys walked along the shore. A flock of ducks honked at them from somewhere overhead.

"I wonder where Big Foot likes to hang out," Nick said.

"He probably stays close to those woods," Riley said. He pointed to a line of trees that led into another forest. "They're close to the water. He can hide there, then sneak out for a quick drink, and sneak back in."

"Do they eat fish?" Nick asked.

"I think they eat *everything*," Riley said.

They walked toward the forest. A large tree trunk had fallen and lay near the lake.

"Let's wait here for Elder Jack," Nick said. He climbed onto the trunk.

Riley paced back and forth in front of him. "What if Big Foot shows up before Elder Jack gets here?"

"They don't attack humans, do they?" Nick asked. "I hope they're not like bears."

"No," Riley said. But Nick thought he didn't look sure about it.

Nick looked back to the trail. He hoped his dad would come walking out.

"It's okay," Riley said.

Nick thought he saw something out of the corner of his eye. He looked toward the trees off to his left. Was something moving?

"What's that?" Riley asked. He had seen something, too.

Both boys strained to see what was there.

Suddenly there was a *roar* right next to them as something big and furry rose up from behind the log. Its arms were raised high.

Nick screamed and leapt off the log. He staggered away from the beast and fell over.

Riley shrieked and ran off.

The *roar* turned into laughter. The beast was Elder Jack dressed in a large furry overcoat and a furry hat that covered most of his face.

"It's all right," he shouted. "It's only me."

Nick wasn't sure if he felt mad or relieved.

Elder Jack crawled over the log and helped Nick to his feet. He chuckled and said, "Where is Riley?"

They looked around.

Elder Jack saw Riley first. He frowned. "Oh," he said.

Nick saw that Riley had run far out onto the ice.

Riley faced them. He saw Elder Jack and started to laugh.

"What are you doing out there?" Elder Jack called out.

It was as if Riley didn't know he was on the ice. "I wasn't paying attention to where I was running," he called back.

Elder Jack went to the edge of the ice and waved his gloved hands in a downward motion. "Don't make any sudden moves. Get down on your belly and slide back to us," he shouted.

"It's okay," Riley said. "The ice is thick."

"Do as I say," Elder Jack said in a stern voice.

Riley took a step toward them. There was a loud *crack*.

"Get down!" Elder Jack shouted. "Spread your weight."

Riley looked down. Water poured around his feet. He took another step as if he hoped to run for it. Suddenly he broke through the ice. He fell from their sight.

"No!" Elder Jack shouted.

Riley popped up again. He screamed and clawed at the ice.

He's going to drown! Nick thought. He was about to go onto the ice after Riley.

Elder Jack grabbed his shoulder

and pulled him back. "You can't. You'll break through."

"We have to do something!" Nick begged.

Elder Jack moved back and forth along the ice. "Calm down, Riley. Float! Don't thrash! Use your arms and body weight to get onto the ice! Paddle with your legs!"

Riley was too busy screaming to listen.

Elder Jack spun to Nick. "Watch him. Tell him what I said. I have to find a long branch. Or rope. I have rope in my truck."

Nick watched helplessly as Elder Jack dashed to the woods.

Riley screamed and sputtered, "Help!" He bobbed up and down in the pool of water.

Nick cupped his hands around his mouth and shouted, "Be calm! Float! Don't splash! Climb onto the ice!

Kick your legs to push yourself out of the water!"

It was no good.

Nick's brain felt frozen. All he could think was: *Jesus, Mary, and Joseph— help!* over and over.

Riley went under again. Nick reached for him. He stepped onto the ice, then stepped back again.

Riley popped up again and thrashed even more.

He's going to tire himself out, Nick thought.

"It's cold! I can't feel my legs!" Riley said. He clawed at the ice more frantically and slipped backward. Down he went.

Nick looked to the woods. Elder Jack was nowhere to be seen. Panic filled his heart and mind. *I can't let him drown,* Nick thought. *I have to do something!*

He kept shouting for Riley to calm down and pull himself onto the ice.

He thought about what Elder Jack had said. *Get down, spread your weight.*

Riley went under again.

Then he had an idea. If he held onto one sleeve and threw the other sleeve to Riley, he could pull him out. He took off his coat and wrapped the end of a sleeve around his hand. He lay down on the ice. He could feel the cold and wet through his thick sweater. He began to crawl on the ice with his elbows like a soldier.

Riley saw Nick. He seemed to calm down a little.

"Use your legs to kick yourself onto the ice!" Nick shouted at him.

For the first time, Riley seemed to understand. He tried to bounce onto the ice with the top of his body. The ice broke away.

"It keeps breaking! My arms are numb!" Riley cried out.

Nick slid closer and closer.

"I'm going to throw my coat at you,"

Nick yelled. "Grab it! I'll pull you out!"

Riley went down again, then up with more sputtering.

Nick was close enough to throw his coat. It landed in front of Riley.

"Grab it!" Nick shouted.

Riley reached for it. He caught hold of the sleeve with one hand.

"Hold on!" Nick said.

Riley kicked and grabbed the sleeve with his other hand.

Nick rolled back and pulled at his coat. Riley held on. He came further up out of the water. The ice cracked.

Nick rolled and pulled harder. A flash of pain shot through his left wrist. He cried out but held onto his coat. Riley was coming out.

The ice cracked more. A line moved like lightning between Riley and Nick. Then the ice gave way.

Nick and Riley both dropped into the water.

The shock of cold stunned Nick. He forced himself upright. Riley was only a few feet away. He screamed again. Nick still had hold of his coat and threw it onto the ice. Riley still had the other end. Nick turned toward the shore. *I have to get there,* he thought.

He pushed himself. Then his feet touched something hard. He put his foot down. It was solid ground. He planted his other foot and stood up.

The water came up to his waist.

He turned to Riley, who was still thrashing in the water.

"Stand up!" he shouted and yanked at his coat.

Riley looked at Nick.

"Stand up!" Nick shouted again. He reached down and grabbed Riley by the collar. "Come on." He gave a hard tug.

Riley struggled to get to his feet.

Together the two boys labored to the shore. They fell onto the hard ground. Nick panted. Riley coughed and sputtered next to him.

The cold felt like it had gone past Nick's skin and deep into his bones.

He heard the sound of a motor. Twisting around, he saw an old pickup truck coming toward them. He also heard shouts from a familiar voice. His father was running in their direction.

CHAPTER FIFTEEN

Tea & Sympathy

Nick and Riley were wrapped in blankets and put into Elder Jack's pickup truck. The heat was turned up high. They drove down a service road to the building site.

Nick sat and shivered. His dad pulled him close and rubbed his arms and chest and legs. He thought about the other times he'd had to ride home after an accident. More than normal, he guessed.

"That was dangerous," Elder Jack said from the driver's seat. He apologized again and again for scaring the boys.

"I don't know why I ran onto the ice," Riley said through chattering teeth. "I thought I was going to drown."

The water only came up to my waist, Nick kept thinking.

His wrist hurt. He took off his wet gloves and pulled up his sleeve. His wrist looked red and seemed bigger than usual.

"Does it hurt?" his dad asked.

Nick nodded.

"We'll have it looked at," his dad said. He took out his cell phone and called Uncle Clark at the building site.

Uncle Clark was ready when they arrived. He had dry clothes that were way too big for the boys, more blankets, and hot tea. They sat in the big trailer-office. Nick thought the hot tea was the best he'd ever tasted.

"Riley, can I call your parents?" Uncle Clark asked him.

"My dad doesn't have a cell phone," Riley said.

"How about a house or office phone?" Uncle Clark said.

Riley shook his head. "Just take me back to the house. My dad will pick me up at three o'clock from there."

Nick looked at his father.

His father said, "It would be better for me to take you home now and explain what happened."

"It's okay," Riley said. That was the end of the conversation.

Nick was puzzled. *Why doesn't Riley want to go home?*

"What about Big Foot?" Riley asked Elder Jack. "Can we go back to see?"

Elder Jack shook his head. "All that noise would have scared him away."

When the boys were warm and dry, Nick's dad drove them back to the Perry house. They sat near the fireplace in the family room. Mrs. Perry put their clothes in the dryer and hung their coats and gloves by the roaring fire. They had more hot tea.

They put ice on Nick's wrist—which seemed kind of funny to Nick, since ice caused the problem. His wrist still hurt.

Mrs. Perry and Sam hovered nearby.

Sam asked the boys a lot of questions. *What were you thinking when you crashed through the ice?* and *Did you*

think you were gonna die? and *How cold was the water?*

Mrs. Perry told Sam to leave the boys alone.

Riley's father came at three o'clock just like Riley had said. The clothes were dry by then.

Riley said, "I'll go out. Thanks for everything!"

"I want to meet your father," Mr. Perry said.

Riley stammered, "He's shy. He doesn't like to meet people."

Mr. Perry stepped out onto the porch and waved for Riley's dad to come in.

Mr. Switzer came to the door. He had red hair that stuck out in different places. He wore tan-colored grease-stained overalls and worn-out work boots. He hunched a little.

Nick realized that Riley's dad was the man who helped serve food at the soup kitchen.

Nick looked at Riley. Riley looked at the floor.

Mr. Perry explained what happened at the Little Big Pond. Mr. Switzer listened and then nodded. He mumbled, "Boys will be boys." He shook Mr. Perry's hand. Then he shook Nick's hand and said, "Thank you for keeping my boy alive." He put a hand on Riley's shoulder and they left.

Nick looked out the window. Riley and his father got into a small white car with gray tape covering one of the windows. Rusted spots dotted the corners of the doors.

They must be poor, Nick thought. *Is that why Riley didn't want to go straight home?*

Nick went back to the fireplace. Mr. Perry sat down next to him and talked in soft tones about the dangers of what happened. "You took a big risk going in after Riley," his dad said.

"But the water wasn't deep," Nick said.

"You didn't know that," his dad said. "There are a lot of sad stories about people drowning while trying to help someone else."

Nick nodded. *Maybe it was stupid,* he thought. "But I couldn't just stand there," he said.

"You were clever to think of using your coat," his dad said. "But it was still very dangerous. It would have been better to wait. We could have lost you today."

He looked up into his father's eyes. They were wet with tears.

"But I couldn't let him drown," Nick said.

Mr. Perry wrapped his arms around Nick and sighed deeply. "I know."

Nick's mom brought in a tray of more hot drinks.

Nick thought for a moment. "Are Riley and his dad poor?" he asked his parents.

Mrs. Perry sat down next to Nick. "Riley's dad helps at the soup kitchen. They eat there a lot. I think they're staying in one of the rooms upstairs."

"Why?" Nick asked. "Where is Riley's mom?"

"She died a few years ago," she said. "Riley's dad couldn't cope very well. He left town. I guess he came back a few months ago and hasn't been able to find a job."

"What does he do?" Mr. Perry asked.

"He is a mechanic," said Mrs. Perry.

"I'll talk to Clark," Mr. Perry said. "Maybe he needs help up at the building site."

Nick hoped so. He felt bad that Riley was poor.

Uncle Clark showed up later. Nick's dad talked to him about Donald Switzer. Uncle Clark promised to find work for him.

"I can use a good mechanic," Uncle Clark said.

Uncle Clark then announced that he had something to show them. Everyone sat down together in the family room. Uncle Clark sat next to Nick on the sofa.

"Nick, while you were at the Big Little Pond, one of my workers saw something in the woods," Uncle Clark said. He reached into the inside pocket of his sports jacket and pulled out an envelope. "He grabbed his phone and took some pictures. He only had a couple of seconds, so they're blurry."

He opened the flap of the envelope and carefully took out three printed photos.

Nick sat on the edge of the seat. "What is it?"

Uncle Clark spread the photos on the coffee table. Nick knelt down for a closer look. He saw trees and snow. Then he saw behind the trees something that looked like a very tall man. Or it might have been a skinny bear. He wasn't sure. It was big and furry all over. It was slightly turned away so he couldn't see a face.

Uncle Clark pointed to the pictures. "It's clearest in this one. Then it moves away into the trees and seems to disappear."

Nick gasped. "Is that Big Foot?" he asked.

Uncle Clark shrugged. "I don't know."

The whole family moved in for a better look.

Nick's heart pounded. It sure looked like Big Foot.

"Are you sure it isn't a joke?" Sam's dad asked.

"The man who took the photos isn't a practical joker," Uncle Clark said. "I told Elder Jack. He found the tracks. The feet were twice the size of a human's."

Sam looked at the blurry furry figure. "It's real?" she asked.

Uncle Clark gazed at her. "There are a lot of great mysteries in the world that we may never figure out."

CHAPTER SIXTEEN

Palms & Kings

The next morning was Palm Sunday. Nick woke up to pain in his wrist.

"We may have to take you to the clinic," Mrs. Perry said.

Mr. Perry found a splint in their first aid cupboard. He wrapped Nick's wrist up. Then he put Nick's arm in a sling so his wrist pointed up to his right shoulder.

"Why?" Nick asked.

"That'll keep the swelling down," his dad said.

Nick wiggled his fingers. His wrist didn't hurt as much.

Mrs. Perry stayed home with Lizzy. The rest of the Perry family went to Palm Sunday Mass.

Everyone met outside of the church. The sun shone bright, but there was a cold edge to the air. Father Cliff and Deacon Chuck wore bright red vestments.

Nick had forgotten that the Mass began with a parade. Everyone waved palm fronds. Deacon Chuck read the story about how Jesus rode the young donkey into Jerusalem and everyone shouted "Hosanna!" Then they moved into the church.

This Mass had the long reading of the Passion of the Lord. Father Cliff, Deacon Chuck, and Uncle Clark read the parts.

The parishioners read the parts for the crowd. Nick felt a funny kind of pain when they shouted "Crucify him!" He felt like he was really doing it. He looked over at Sam. She had tears in her eyes.

The long reading ended with Jesus dying on the Cross.

"To be continued," Andrew whispered.

The church served coffee and donuts after the Mass.

Nick thought he had seen Brad when they first arrived. Brad's parents were sitting at a table in the meeting area.

"Where's Brad?" he asked them.

"He's somewhere around here," Brad's mother said.

Nick went down one hall and then another.

He's probably playing games again, Nick thought.

He found Brad sitting in one of the church rooms for children. The walls were lined with shelves of toys. Brad sat on a chair and fiddled with a toy that looked like a cell phone with really big buttons.

"Hey," Nick said.

"Hey," Brad said. Nick could tell he was in a bad mood.

"What's wrong?" asked Nick.

Brad put the toy on the table. "We had to stand for *fifteen* minutes while they read that really *long* Bible story."

Nick didn't know what to say. He had never heard anyone complain about hearing the story of how Jesus died.

"It's Palm Sunday. Next Sunday is Easter. We're supposed to hear that story," Nick finally said.

Brad gave a loud grunt.

"What's wrong with you?" Nick asked.

He kicked his foot against the leg of the table. "My parents caught me playing a game. They took *all* my stuff away for a *month*. That's not even Lent anymore."

Nick thought about saying "I told you so" but didn't.

"Now we have a whole week of *this*." He waved his hand. Nick knew that *this* meant church. By *church* Brad meant the Holy Week services. There were a few of them this week.

"Why does the Catholic Church make everything so hard?" Brad said. "I have friends that go to other churches and they don't give up things for Lent. They don't *have* Lent."

Nick couldn't imagine a church that didn't have Lent.

Brad kept talking, "They don't even have to go to church every week."

Nick was confused. "They don't go to church? How can they be Christian and not go to church?"

Brad shrugged. "And when they go to church, it's *fun*. People sing and play guitars and drums. It's like a concert. It's not boring like ours."

Nick thought about what to say. Then a shadow fell near them. Nick turned around. Deacon Chuck Crosby had come in the door.

Deacon Chuck was now wearing his white deacon's robe. He had bushy white hair on his head and a round face. His eyes always looked like they were smiling. The kids liked Deacon Chuck. He often told jokes and stories.

"Is everything alright?" Deacon Chuck asked.

Brad looked up but didn't say anything.

"Brad thinks church is boring," Nick said.

Brad glared at Nick.

Deacon Chuck pulled a chair over and sat down next to the two boys.

"I suppose church can be boring if you're not going for the right reasons," Deacon Chuck said.

"I go because my parents make me," Brad said.

"That's probably true for a lot of kids," Deacon Chuck said. "But you're here at school because your parents make you, right?"

Brad nodded.

"Your parents make you do a lot of things that are good for you. Church is one of them," Deacon Chuck said.

Brad frowned. "It wouldn't be so bad if the Mass was more fun."

Deacon Chuck thought for a moment.

"I have a story that might help," he said. Nick grabbed another chair and sat down.

This is the story Deacon Chuck told:

Once upon a time there was a king who loved the people of his kingdom more than anything else in the world. This king often left his castle to help his people. Together they built homes to live in and barns for their animals. He helped farmers who were injured to plow their fields. He visited the sick in the hospitals. He helped parents with their newborn babies. He made sure the schools taught everyone well. He settled fights and complaints. He also gave them great festivals and circuses with acrobats and jugglers and singers and dancers and food and games.

The people were grateful. They said to the king, "What can we do to give you thanks?"

The king said, "Come to the great hall in my castle. Let us meet together in peace. Put aside your worries. Let us forgive each other our offenses. We will spend time together as a family. We will share joy. I will teach you all the great things I know. That is how you can show your thanks."

So every week the people came to the castle. They made peace. They forgave each other. The king shared his wisdom with them. He gave them hope and beauty and truth. They were like a family.

As time went on, the people became restless. They forgot that their time with the king was to say thank you for all the wonderful things he did for them. They stopped listening to his wisdom. They wanted their time with him to be like one of the great festivals with acrobats and jugglers and singers and dancers.

One day the leaders went to the king. They told him the people were not happy. They said what the people wanted.

The king listened patiently. Then he said to the leaders, "Our time is not supposed to be like a circus. It is not supposed to be like anything else you do in your life. Fun things do not last. They are here for a moment and then go away. We are meant to live for something greater. Your time with me will feed your very souls. It will give you life long after your fun and your homes and your crops have gone away."

The leaders reported to the people. They grumbled. Many stopped going to the castle to meet the king. Some went but got annoyed by their time with him. Even though he still helped them with many of their needs, they stopped giving him thanks in the way he wanted.

Deacon Chuck looked at the two boys. "What do you think the king should do with his people?"

Nick and Brad looked at one another. They didn't say anything.

Deacon Chuck smiled at them. "Give it some thought." He stood up. "I have to get ready for the next Mass." He strolled out.

"We go to Mass to say thanks," Nick said.

Brad grumbled, "I don't want to talk about it anymore."

Just then Brad's parents appeared in the doorway. "There you are. We're ready to go."

Brad stood up. He left with his parents.

Nick stayed behind. He thought about the story. He didn't know what the king should do. He thought, *If I were the king, I would stop helping the people because they were ungrateful.*

He thought about it some more.

It's a good thing I'm not the king, he decided.

Nick's father didn't like the color or size of Nick's left wrist.

"I want to be sure you didn't re-break it," he said.

At two o'clock Nick and his dad were sitting in an urgent care clinic. A half-hour after that Dr. Maggie Duriez heard the story of how he'd hurt his wrist.

She turned his wrist this way and that. "Were you doing your stretches and exercises?" she asked.

Nick looked at his father.

"Have you?" he asked.

"Not really," Nick said.

"That might explain why you're here today," she said.

She sent him to another room to have X-rays done.

A little while later the doctor came in. She announced, "The good news is that your wrist isn't broken."

Nick was glad.

"But you've sprained it," she said. "You'll have to continue what you've been doing: rest it, keep it compressed in the splint, and wear the sling to keep it above your heart."

Nick's dad had a playful smile on his face. "Would he have this problem if he'd been doing his wrist exercises?"

Dr. Duriez said, "A stronger wrist is more resistant to strains and sprains."

"I thought so," Mr. Perry said with a sharp look at his son.

CHAPTER SEVENTEEN

Rights & Wrongs

Sam usually looked forward to Holy Week. But this one was muddled by the final spelling bee on Wednesday.

She was given the list of words on Monday. She stared at the hundred possible choices. Some of them she already knew how to spell. She wasn't so sure about the others. A lot of them looked really *big*.

Her classmates—"Team Sam"—kept saying things like "you'll win" and "put

Karl in his place" and "we know you can do it." She didn't feel better.

She watched her coat and her desk and her backpack. If the mystery word-giver had put a list in any of them, she didn't see it.

Why did I say yes to this spelling bee? she kept asking herself.

Nick felt like he'd lost all his friends.

Brad seemed to be ignoring him, and he didn't know why.

Riley kept acting like he didn't have any time to talk.

They're only an arm's reach away, Nick thought. *How can they both avoid me?*

But they did.

Nick mused about it all morning. He couldn't think what he'd done wrong.

"You can't quit now," Kim said to Sam during recess.

They were standing under the large maple tree in the schoolyard. Or maybe it was oak. Sam wasn't sure. She spelled the two words in her head. *Does "Maple" have one "p" or two?* she wondered.

She shook her head. "I can't handle it."

Kim sat down on a big root of the tree. "You've worked so hard. You've come this far. You can't stop now. That would be like ... like going thirty-eight days in Lent without eating a hamburger. And then you eat one on the thirty-ninth day."

Sam didn't say anything. Her mind went to a big fat juicy hamburger.

"You haven't eaten a hamburger, have you?" Kim asked.

"No," said Sam. "But what if I fail?"

"Then go to Confession," said Kim.

"I mean, what if I fail the spelling bee?" Sam clarified.

Kim shook her head. "You won't fail."

"What if I do?" Sam asked.

"Then you fail. Who cares?" said Kim.

"*Everybody!*" Sam said with a small cry.

Kim put her arm around Sam. "You're only a failure if you fail to try."

Sam looked at her. "Fortune cookie?" she asked.

"Yeah," said Kim. "I saw it the other day at my cousin's restaurant."

Sam groaned. "Aren't there any *Bible* verses about winning a spelling bee?"

Kim thought about it. "Jesus talked about the *Bee*-attitudes," she offered.

"*You're not helping,*" Sam said.

Sam sat in her room. She thought she might cry.

Her mom was helping at the soup kitchen. Her dad had gone off to meet Uncle Clark about something.

What can I do?

She asked Nick to help her practice spelling the words. He was in a dark mood and kept messing up the words.

"L-A-F-F" he said for "laugh" and "N-E-W-Z-P-A-P-E-R" for "newspaper."

"What are you doing?" Sam asked him.

"Do you ever get the feeling that you've done something wrong but you don't know what?" Nick asked her.

"I will after the spelling bee," she said.

She gave up and went to Andrew. He was in the family room looking at a big book with a lot of black and white pictures.

"Did you know that President Theodore Roosevelt came to Hope Springs?" Andrew said. "He came through on a train and stayed at the hotel. They nearly had riots from people trying to get close to him."

"Oh," Sam said. She remembered that Theodore Roosevelt was the president with the big bushy mustache. She didn't know what else to say, so she asked, "Will you help me with my spelling bee words?"

He closed the book. "Okay."

They were just about to start when Nick came in. "I don't understand my friends," he announced.

"What's wrong with them?" Andrew asked.

Nick began to talk about Brad and Riley and how they avoided him at school.

Sam gave up and went back to her room. She had a science worksheet to do.

"'S-I-E-N-C-E'" she spelled out loud.

She reached into her backpack and took out her science folder. The word was written on the front. She sighed. "I forgot the first 'C'."

She opened the folder. A folded piece of paper was on the inside.

Sam thought her heart skipped a beat.

Open it, she thought. *Just take a quick look.*

She picked up the sheet.

Maybe it isn't what you think it is.

She turned it over in her hands.

"I hope you win" was written on an outside fold.

She started to unfold the sheet. She stopped.

This is cheating, she told herself.

She sat the sheet down on her desk.

The thoughts raced through her mind. *This is what I need to win. My classmates will be proud. I'll be their hero.*

She picked up the sheet again. Her fingers moved beneath the first fold and flipped it over. Now she was looking at the sheet folded in half.

I need this. This will help me win. I'll be a hero.

She closed her eyes.

No, she thought. She tossed the sheet to the side of her desk. Then she picked it up again and threw it in the trash can.

There! she thought.

Lizzy was sitting up in her bed when Sam stepped into her room. She had her sketch pad on her lap. It was the first time Sam had seen her draw in a few weeks. Lizzy loved to draw.

"You must be feeling better," Sam said.

"A little," Lizzy said.

Sam said, "I'll bet it's been hard being cooped up in your room all this time."

"I don't mind," Lizzy said.

"But being alone is so *lonely*," Sam said. She sat down on the edge of the bed.

"I haven't been alone," Lizzy said.

Sam looked at Lizzy and tried to guess what she meant. She asked, "Do you mean your guardian angel?"

"My guardian angel," she said. "And Mary. And the saints. And Jesus."

Sam turned to the room. She almost imagined that it was crowded with all of those people.

Lizzy held up her drawing.

Sam saw figures that looked like

Jesus and Mary and women and men in robes like they wore in the Bible.

Lizzy tapped the sketch pad. "They're all here."

"Do you see them?" Sam asked.

Lizzy went on sketching. "They were in a dream I had last night."

Sam gazed at her sister for a moment. "You are so strange."

"In a good way or a bad way?" Lizzy asked.

"All good," said Sam. Then she decided to tell Lizzy about the spelling bee list—the one with the words circled.

Lizzy put her sketch pad and pencil aside. "Where is it?" she asked.

"I threw it away."

"It's in your trash can?" Lizzy asked.

"Uh huh," she replied. She felt proud of herself.

"That was a good first step," Lizzy said.

"*First* step?" said Sam.

"Did you tear it up?" Lizzy asked.

"No."

"So it's sitting there, just waiting for you to pick it up again," said Lizzy.

"But I won't," Sam said.

Lizzy raised her eyebrows. "It'll be there all night. And tomorrow. And tomorrow night. And you'll be thinking how strong you are for resisting it. But it'll keep tempting you until you decide it's easier to look at the answers."

Sam sat very still.

"It's a trick we all play on ourselves to prove that we're strong," Lizzy said. "It's better to know we're weak."

"Should I tear it up?" she asked her sister.

"Bring it to me. I'll give it to Mom. Mom can give it to Sister Lucy," Lizzy said.

Sam went to her room. She picked up the trash can and carried it back into Lizzy's room. "I don't want to touch it," Sam said.

Lizzy reached in and pulled out the folded paper. She looked closely at it. "Sister Lucy will know that handwriting," she said.

Sam hugged her sister. "Thank you for being a good kind of strange."

CHAPTER EIGHTEEN

Friends & Feuds

Mrs. Perry and Sam took the word list to Sister Lucy the next morning.

"You promise me that you didn't look at it?" Sister Lucy asked Sam.

"I promise."

"None of us opened it up," Mrs. Perry added. "Lizzy slept with it under her pillow."

Sister Lucy held the paper away from her with two fingers. "She has mono, doesn't she?"

"She's not contagious anymore," Mrs. Perry said.

"I'm glad," Sister Lucy said. She looked at the handwritten note. "I know who wrote this."

"Who?" Sam asked.

Sister Lucy put the sheet in the top drawer of her desk and closed it. She put on a wry smile. "I'll tell you after the spelling bee tomorrow."

Nick was fed up. Brad was still ignoring him. Riley wouldn't look at him.

He fumed about it all morning. What had he done wrong?

He decided to confront them.

He looked for Brad at lunch. Brad wasn't there. Neither was Riley.

Are they having lunch together? Nick wondered.

He went outside at recess. He saw Riley standing by the bench next to the playground.

Riley saw Nick coming and looked like he was about to walk away.

Nick caught his arm. "Wait a minute," Nick said. "Are you mad at me?"

"No," Riley said.

"Then what's wrong?" Nick asked.

Riley looked down at his feet. He shuffled them back and forth. Then he said, "I don't like how you look at me."

Nick frowned, then he tried to stop frowning so he wouldn't look like he was frowning. "How do I look at you?" he asked.

"Like you saved my life," Riley said.

"What?" Nick asked.

"I feel stupid because I could have stood up and walked out of the ice," Riley said.

"You didn't know," said Nick.

Riley shook his head. "I could have put my feet down."

"You were panicked," Nick said.

"I was stupid," Riley said.

Nick groaned.

Riley shuffled his feet some more and said, "I don't want you to feel sorry for me."

"Why would I feel sorry for you?" Nick asked.

Riley glanced around to make sure no one was listening. "Because you saw us at the soup kitchen. You saw my dad. You know we're poor."

"Now you *are* being stupid," Nick said. He tried not to sound mean. "I'm sorry you and your dad are having trouble. But I don't feel sorry for you."

Riley looked like he didn't believe Nick. "Then why did your dad come to see my dad at the soup kitchen?" he asked.

Nick was surprised. "He did? When?"

Riley glanced around again. "Last night. He and your mom talked to my dad in the office at the soup kitchen."

"I didn't know that," Nick said.

Riley shoved his hands into his coat. *"We don't want your help."*

Nick spread his arms. "I'm not giving you any help!"

"Good!" said Riley.

"Good!" said Nick.

The two boys stood in a stubborn silence.

Nick looked at Riley for a minute. "Do you *need* help?"

Riley dropped down on the bench. He looked frustrated. "Are you any good at history?" he asked.

Nick sat down next to him. "A little," he said.

"I need help studying for our test next week."

"We can study together after school," Nick said.

Riley nudged Nick with his elbow. "Thanks."

"Ow," said Nick.

Riley had nudged his left arm.

The bell rang for the end of school. Nick went to the closet to get his coat. He took it off the hook and nearly ran into Brad as he came around the corner.

"Watch out," Brad said.

"What's wrong? Why are you mad at me?" Nick asked.

Brad grabbed his coat. "I'm not mad at you."

"You're acting mad," Nick insisted.

Brad put on his coat and said, "I don't want to get in the way of your *new* best friend.

Nick frowned. "What new best friend?"

"Big Foot," he said and nodded towards Riley's empty desk. "Since you saved his *life* at the lake. You two are having all kinds of adventures now."

"I wanted you to go with us," Nick said. "You said it was a waste of time."

"Forget it." Brad walked away.

Nick followed him. "Tell me what you're talking about," he demanded.

Brad spun around. "Just stay away from me."

"*Why?*" Nick asked.

Brad leaned close to Nick. So close Nick thought he smelled licorice on Brad's breath. "It's *your* fault my parents took my games away," Brad said.

Nick was stunned. "How is it *my* fault?"

"Because you kept telling me to stop," Brad said. "You probably *prayed* that my parents would find out, just to stop me."

"I didn't pray about that," Nick said. "But you *should have* stopped on your own. You made a promise. It was wrong to break it."

"Yeah, just like you were supposed to do your wrist exercises," Brad sneered. "You're not such a saint."

Nick lifted his arm in the sling. "Look what that got me."

Brad grunted. "And you made Deacon Chuck tell us that story. And I had to tell my parents because they saw him come out of the classroom. Now my parents want us to go to *every* Mass this week."

"That's not my fault," said Nick.

"Yes, it is," Brad said.

Nick looked at his friend. He didn't know what to say. Finally he growled, "I think you're going crazy."

Brad scowled at him. "I think you should leave me alone." He stormed away. "I wish I didn't go to this school!" he shouted.

Nick stood where he was.

I don't understand people sometimes, he thought.

Sam rubbed her eyes. The list of spelling words were getting jumbled together.

"It's time for bed," her mother said.

Sam had been sitting in the family room. The list was resting in her lap. Her school work was scattered on the couch around her.

"Bed," Sam repeated. "B-E-D."

Mrs. Perry laughed. "Now," she said. "N-O-W."

Sam gathered up her papers. "Can you write me a note?"

"For what?" her mother asked.

"To excuse me from the spelling bee," Sam said.

Mrs. Perry picked up the list. "You know these words. You've always been a good speller."

"I'm tired," Sam said. She felt like crying.

"Do you want me to call Sister Lucy?" her mother said.

Sam fell over onto the couch. *C-O-U-C-H*, she thought.

Her mother moved Sam's legs aside and sat down next to her. She gently moved Sam's hair away from her face. "I will if you're serious," she said.

Sam took a deep breath. "No. It's too late now anyway."

"We can pray about it," her mom said.

Sam looked at her hopefully. "For me to win?"

"For you to finish well," Mrs. Perry said. "We often fall just when we're within reach. A voice tells us we can't do it, we're too tired, we don't have the strength. That voice is wrong."

"It *sounds* right," Sam said. She yawned.

Mrs. Perry softly rubbed Sam's arm. "Tonight we'll pray for God to give you the strength to finish well. And we'll pray for you to be gracious whether you win or lose."

CHAPTER NINETEEN

Betrayals & Breakers

Father Cliff's address in the Wednesday morning assembly was about Judas. He reminded everyone that Judas met with the leaders who wanted to arrest and kill Jesus. Then Judas went to the Last Supper and sat at the table like he was friends with Jesus.

"As we come to these last few days of Lent, I hope we'll remember who we are in this story," Father Cliff said. "When Jesus told the disciples that one of them would betray him, they were all afraid.

'Is it me?' they asked. They realized that it *could* be them. Each one of them had it in his heart to betray Jesus, just like Judas. We all do. Just like we have it in our hearts to deny Jesus, just like Peter."

Father Cliff paused, then asked, "What's the difference between Peter and Judas?"

Sam waited to see if anyone would answer.

Father Cliff didn't wait. "Judas realized what he had done and felt sorry for himself. He couldn't see beyond his sin. He couldn't believe in God's grace. So he ended it all. He took himself out of the race because he was looking down, not up."

Sam turned and looked back at her mom a few rows behind her. Did she know Father Cliff was going to talk about this? Her mom was watching Father Cliff.

"What about Peter?" Father Cliff asked. "Peter denied Jesus three times. But he learned something that Judas refused to learn. Peter looked past his own sin. He looked up and saw that God's grace was still there for him. He knew that God could still carry him the rest of the way."

Sam thought about all that Father Cliff was saying.

He continued, "No matter how dark things get, there is always God's light. No matter what kind of terrible 'Good Friday' you have, Sunday is coming. No matter what kind of cross you carry, life is just beyond it. God's love is there when we fail. It's there when we suffer. It's there when we're scared or anxious or stressed. All we have to do is reach out."

Sam remembered her mother's prayer from the night before. "Finish well," she had said.

"Whether I win or lose," Sam whispered.

It was time for the final spelling bee. The first and second graders were done. Sam and Karl took their places at the microphones. Karl smiled at Sam. He looked like he knew something she didn't.

Sister Stephanie tapped her microphone. "I have to officially announce to the monitors that I've changed the words I was going to use this morning."

"What?" Karl hissed. He looked like someone had just punched him.

She handed pages to Mrs. Craft on her left and Mr. Landers on her right.

Sister Stephanie said to Karl and Sam, "It won't make a difference, since neither of you were supposed to know what words I had originally chosen."

Sam nodded to Sister Stephanie. Karl looked like he'd just been jolted with an electric cord.

Sister Stephanie gave Karl his first word: *Donkey.*

Karl repeated the word and slowly spelled it correctly.

Sam thought he seemed more nervous than ever before.

Her first word was *Damage.*

Sam repeated the word and spelled "D-A-M-A-G-E."

"Correct," Sister Stephanie said. She went back and forth between the two contestants. *Jury, Betray, Hosanna...*

Karl struggled with the word "Hosanna" but got it right in the end.

Both spelled their five words correctly.

"It's a tie," Sister Stephanie said. "So we now have to come up with words that'll work as tie-breakers. Ready?"

Sam and Karl waited.

"Samantha, the word is 'Wednesday,'" she said.

Sam's eyes widened. *Wednesday. Why did it have to be Wednesday?*

Sam swallowed hard. "Please use it in a sentence."

Some of the kids in the audience chuckled.

Sister Stephanie said, "The day after Tuesday is Wednesday."

Sam tried to form the letters in her mind. She looked out at the crowd. Her mom was there, with her father, Andrew, Nick, and Lizzy.

Lizzy is well enough to be here.

"Samantha, please give your spelling," Sister Stephanie said.

Sam closed her eyes for a second and prayed, *Give me a clear mind. Help me finish well.*

"W-E-D-N-E-S-D-A-Y," Sam said.

Sister Stephanie smiled. "That is correct." She turned to Karl and said, "Karl, your word is *Resurrect.*"

Karl got that smirk on his face. "Easy," he said. "Resurrect. R-E-S-S-U-R-E-C-T."

Sister Stephanie looked down at the page in front of her and up at Karl again. "That is wrong. I'm sorry."

Karl's face turned red. "No, it isn't!"

"R-E-S-U-R-R-E-C-T is the correct spelling," Sister Stephanie said.

"That's what I said!" Karl cried out.

Sister Stephanie turned to Mrs. Craft and Mr. Landers. They shook their heads.

"I'm sorry, Karl," she said. "Thank you both for doing so well. Congratulations, Samantha Perry."

The audience applauded. Karl stomped off of the stage. Sam gave a little bow and dashed off in the other direction. She stood behind the stage curtain and tried to keep from fainting.

After the rest of the grades had finished the spelling bee, Sam was given a trophy. Her family hugged her while her father took a photo on his cell phone.

Sister Lucy asked Sam and Mrs. Perry to come to the school office. They walked through to Sister Stephanie's office.

Lance Smith sat in one of the visitor's chairs. Lance's mother stood near the window.

Karl Enslow sat in the other chair. His mother sat on a small sofa along the wall.

Both mothers looked unhappy.

Sister Stephanie stood behind her desk. She gestured for Mrs. Perry to sit down.

"I'll stand, if that's all right," she said. "You sit down, Sam."

Sam sat down on the small sofa next to Karl's mother.

Sister Lucy stepped forward and held up the spelling bee word list with the circles and the handwritten note. "Sam, your mystery helper has been Lance."

Sam gaped at Lance.

Lance gave her a sheepish smile and wiggled his fingers in a little wave.

His mother cleared her throat and he sat up straight.

Sister Lucy said, "Lance and Karl have been friends since Kindergarten. Lance went to Karl's house one Saturday before the spelling bee contest started. He found out that Karl's mom was the one who led Sister Stephanie to the website for the spelling bee words to use."

Sam tried to follow what Sister Lucy was saying. *Karl's mom found the spelling bee website with the words Sister Stephanie used for the contest. Lance found out about it. Got it.*

"What else did you find out?" Sister Lucy asked Lance.

Lance cleared his throat loudly and said, "I found out that Karl could get on the website and look at the answers. He was going to cheat to win the spelling bee."

Karl lowered his head. He shot a hard look at Lance.

"So what did you do, Lance?" Sister Stephanie asked the boy.

"I found out how to get on the website, too. So I printed out the list to help Sam," Lance said. "It seemed only fair. Especially because I love her."

"*Lance!*" Mrs. Smith snapped.

"Like a friend, I mean," Lance added quickly.

"It was still cheating," Sister Lucy reminded him.

"Yeah, it was," Lance admitted.

"Mrs. Smith and Mrs. Enslow have confirmed it all," Sister Lucy said.

"It's true," said Mrs. Smith.

"There will be consequences," said Mrs. Enslow.

Sam had to wonder what the consequences would be.

"I'm very sorry," said Mrs. Enslow. "So is Karl."

Karl didn't look very sorry.

"I'm sorry, too," said Lance.

Mrs. Smith said she was sorry Lance behaved so badly.

That was the end of the meeting. And the mystery.

"You never looked at the answers?" Sister Lucy asked Sam again later.

"No. I wanted to. But I didn't," Sam said.

Sister Lucy put an arm around Sam. "You're stronger than I was at your age," she whispered.

CHAPTER TWENTY

Holy & Helpful

The Sacred Triduum was the series of celebrations that led up to Easter Sunday.

They began on Thursday with an evening Mass. The Perry family went together. As they sat down, Nick looked around for his friends. He saw that Brad was there with his family. Brad looked miserable.

He also saw Riley sitting with his father. Riley was in his school uniform. His father still wore his stained overalls.

Part of the Mass remembered how Jesus washed the feet of his disciples at the Last Supper to show his love for them. Jesus said, "I give you a new commandment to love one another as I have loved you."

Chairs and bowls of water were brought out. Father Cliff, Deacon Chuck, and a handful of other men gathered near the altar. The ushers asked various members of the parish to have their feet washed by the leaders of the church.

Riley and his father were asked to come forward. Riley's father looked startled and unsure. Riley took his hand and led him to Father Cliff, who told them to sit down in the chairs. He then took off their shoes and socks. He slowly washed their feet in the bowl and then carefully dried them with a towel. Riley and his father stood up. Riley picked up his shoes and socks.

His father suddenly hugged Father Cliff.

"Thank you," he said. He grabbed his shoes and socks and nearly ran back to where they'd been sitting.

Nick thought he saw tears in the eyes of Riley's father.

Nick's dad leaned over and whispered, "He starts work tomorrow morning."

Nick looked up at his dad. "Where?"

"Your Uncle Clark has hired him to take care of all the trucks up at the building site," his dad whispered.

Nick looked over at Riley.

Riley was smiling.

The Thursday Mass ended with the Transfer of the Most Blessed Sacrament. The servers stripped the altar of its cross, the candles, and the cloth. Nick felt funny to see it look so abandoned.

Father Cliff was dressed in special robes to lift up a giant gold monstrance. There was incense and large candles and a song as a procession made its way to a large side room. Men dressed like guards held up swords and stood watch.

Everyone took turns to go in to give thanks for the Body and Blood of Jesus.

The room was dark and silent, even though it was full of people kneeling and praying.

Nick knelt down next to Sam. He thought of the story Deacon Chuck had told about the king and his ungrateful people. He now knew the answer to the question: the king showed his love to his people even though their hearts weren't grateful.

The words *make my heart truly grateful* came to his mind like a prayer. He wasn't sure where the words came from.

On Good Friday, the Sacred Triduum continued at three o'clock with the Celebration of the Lord's Passion.

The Perrys went together. The Scripture readings talked about the sacrifice of Jesus for the sins of humanity. Then came the dramatic reading by three people of the arrest, trial, and Crucifixion of Jesus. Nick was surprised when his father went forward to read the part of the Narrator. He also felt the same pangs of sadness when he joined the crowd and shouted, "Crucify him! Crucify him!"

After the reading, there was a time of prayer. Then a large wooden cross was brought to the front by Deacon Chuck and a handful of other men. They held it up as the people sang a song about the cross and the salvation of the world.

Then the parishioners went forward for the Adoration of the Cross. Some people knelt before the cross. Some knelt and kissed the wood. Some touched their fingers to their lips and then touched the wood. Some people cried.

Nick saw Brad go forward with his parents. He didn't look miserable this time. He stood and looked up at the cross with a sad expression on his face.

Nick knelt down in front of the cross and took his arm out of the sling so he could touch the wood with both hands. For just a moment, his wrist didn't ache.

The Mass continued with more prayer and then Holy Communion.

By the end, Nick felt tired and a little light-headed.

"I want to cry," Sam whispered as she hugged him.

This time he let her get away with it.

Sam woke up on Holy Saturday with a feeling like something terrible had happened. She sat up in bed and tried to think what it was. Was she late for school? Had she failed the spelling bee?

Her mind went back to the night before. She had knelt in front of the big wooden cross with Lizzy. Lizzy began to weep. She wrapped her arms around the base of the cross and held it close.

Sam wrapped her arms around Lizzy and held *her* close.

Sam didn't know what had come over her. Maybe it was the music. Maybe it was the emotion of all the people. Maybe it was the cross itself, so rough and terrible.

She had seen so many pretty and colorful crucifixes. It was easy to forget about the wounds and the pain. But the giant, ugly cross that stood before her was raw and frightening. It looked like an exclamation point to the word *Death!*

Is this what it felt like? Sam wondered. *Did the disciples wake up on Saturday and feel sick and empty like this?*

She went to her bedroom window. Mr. Gallagher across the street was on a ladder doing something to the gutter on his roof. A car drove by. A dog ran to the edge of a yard and barked at it. Mrs. Collins walked out to her driveway to pick up a newspaper. She was dressed in a bathrobe.

It was so normal. The sun appeared through the clouds. Maybe spring had come. But Sam didn't feel like it. She still felt the darkness from that cross.

Nick rode his bike to the park near his house. The sun was out and he was glad not to have to go to school.

But it didn't feel like Saturday. It didn't feel like any kind of day he knew. He felt like he'd lost something and couldn't get it back.

He brought his bike to a stop.

Brad was sitting at a picnic table. He was working something in his hands. It looked like a game device.

Nick groaned. *Not today.*

"What are you doing?" Nick asked him. He sat down on the opposite side of the table.

Brad didn't look up. "This thing is being stubborn," he said.

"I thought your parents took all your devices away," Nick said.

Brad held up the device. It was a gray rectangle with a screen in the middle and little knobs on the sides. "This one doesn't work."

Nick still wasn't sure what Brad was doing. "You're trying to fix it?"

"Yep."

"Why?" asked Nick.

"So my brother will sell it," he explained. Brad's older brother was well-known for selling things. Half of the Wilkes' garage was filled with stuff to sell. "I decided to get rid of most of my games and gizmos."

"So you can buy something better?" Nick asked.

Brad fiddled with the device again. "So Riley can buy something better."

Nick shook his head as if he didn't hear right. "Riley?"

"He needs the money more than I do. Maybe he can buy some new clothes or something," Brad said.

"How do you know about Riley?" Nick asked.

Brad gave a sideways look at Nick. "My parents used to be friends with Riley's parents. But Riley's mom died and Riley's dad took off. When I told them a kid named Riley Switzer showed up in class, they knew it must be him. My dad found out that Riley's dad didn't have a job and they've been living at the soup kitchen."

"You knew and didn't tell me," Nick said.

"You knew and didn't tell me either," Brad said.

"Is that why you were mad at me?" Nick asked.

Brad gave a little shrug. "I was mad at my parents for taking all my stuff away. But I can't be mad at them or I'll get in bigger trouble. So I was mad at you. If I can't be mad at my best friend, then who can I be mad at?"

"Nobody, I guess," Nick said. "When did you decide all this?"

Brad put the device down again. "Last night."

"At the cross?" Nick asked.

Brad shrugged again. "It was just a big piece of wood," he said. "I don't know why everybody had to get so worked up."

But Nick knew he didn't mean it.

CHAPTER TWENTY-ONE

Alleluia & Amen

St. Clare's had an Easter Vigil on
Saturday night. The Perry family didn't
go this time. Mrs. Perry served at the
soup kitchen. Mr. Perry thought Lizzy
might relapse again. Nick's wrist was
aching. Sam was worn-out from the
stress of the spelling bee. Only Andrew
seemed like his usual self, but he
thought a three-hour service would be
really hard to do.

The family said their own prayers
and played some games and watched a
movie about the life of Jesus.

On Easter morning they put on their best clothes and went to Mass.

"Christ is risen!" the ushers said at the door.

"Christ is risen indeed!" Mr. Perry said, like it was a secret password to get in.

Sam thought the organ sounded bigger and the choir sounded more joyful than ever.

The songs proclaimed that "Jesus Christ is risen today!"

The Gospel reading told about the woman who went to the empty tomb. The confusion about what it meant. The race between Peter and John to check it out. The burial cloths rolled up. But no body. The Jesus they saw die on the Cross had come back from the dead.

Sam nudged Nick and cocked her head to the right. Riley and his father were there. Both had had their hair

cut. Riley's dad wore a suit. Riley wore a new sweater.

Alleluia, alleluia! Sam heard them say and sing.

She saw Kim and her other friends from school. Everyone was smiling.

It was an amazing morning.

The Easter Sunday meal for the Perry family was lamb and various vegetables.

Mrs. Perry surprised Sam with her own special hamburger.

"Lent is over," she said. "I thought you would want one."

Sam took a bite. It was everything a hamburger should taste like. But she put it down and asked for some of the lamb.

"I don't get it," her father said. "You've been waiting for this."

Sam wasn't sure how to explain it.

She said, "I think I liked the *idea* of a hamburger more than eating a hamburger."

"A wise observation," Mr. Perry said. "Though, I think Nick and I like *eating* candy better than the *idea* of candy."

Nick and his father proved it by attacking a bowl of chocolate candy for their dessert all by themselves.

Read *MORE* Adventures of Nick & Sam!